Sabina Ariani

Virtual Affinities

Summary

"We are increasingly connected,
more informed,
more stimulated,
but existentially increasingly alone."

Tonino Cantelmi

" Virtual affinities "

Jordan spends his days immersed in a world of paint and canvas, in a small loft that nestles below street level, a hidden corner of the city where sunlight barely filters through the small, tall windows. His space is an ordered chaos of canvases, brushes, and paint cans scattered everywhere, silent witnesses of his sleepless nights spent painting. To support himself, Jordan works as a freelance illustrator for websites and small independent publications, a job that allows him to express his creativity while still giving him the flexibility to pursue his true passion: painting. His life took an unexpected turn five years ago, when a relationship with a boy his age created an unbridgeable rift with his parents, leading him to a semi-clandestine existence in his current refuge.

Avery, a respected and career-long art critic, by contrast, lives in a luxurious penthouse with breathtaking views of the bay, a place that shines in the sun by day and sparkles with reflected lights at night. Her life seems like a dream to outsiders, but behind closed doors, she fights a battle to free herself from a toxic marriage. Her husband, a successful lawyer with a penchant for extramarital affairs with much younger women, turned out to be not only unfaithful but also violent. Avery's decision to separate was not an easy one, but it is driven by the determination to regain her independence and rediscover who she truly is, beyond luxury and appearances.

Fate decides to intertwine the lives of Jordan and Avery in an unexpected way. They meet for the first time in a world that they both consider an escape from reality: the metaverse. In this parallel universe, Jordan exhibits his works in a virtual gallery, creating a bridge between his bohemian life and the outside world. Avery, seeking refuge from her personal tribulations and a way to reconnect with her lost passions, stumbles upon Jordan's works during an evening of virtual exploration. Their first conversation occurs under the veil of anonymity that only the metaverse can offer, but the connection is immediate.

Avery is struck by the emotional depth of Jordan's work, while he finds in her a critical intelligence and sensitivity that fascinates him. Without knowing the very different worlds from which they come, they begin to share thoughts and dreams, finding mutual comfort and inspiration.

Thoughts and Rebirths

Thursday afternoon: boring and almost motionless, one of those days where time seems to have forgotten to flow. As Avery looks out the large window of his attic, the gray sky and the raindrops that beat incessantly against the glass seem to mirror the turmoil of his thoughts. Every drop, a reminder of the tears held back, of the silent pain he carried in his heart for too long.

"This rain... it seems like it wants to wash everything away, yet I feel emptier than ever," she thinks, wrapping herself tighter in her blue cardigan.

Her mind wanders aimlessly, as if searching for a spark of hope in a day that seems to have so few. "I have to find a way to shake myself, to not let this rain take away the last piece of me," Avery reflects. She knows that remaining helpless will only fuel that sense of helplessness that she has begun to know too well.

Avery, looking for a distraction from her dark thoughts, approaches the computer with the intention of tackling the task, always procrastinated for her, of sorting through the numerous emails accumulated.

"At least this way I keep myself busy and don't think..." she murmurs to herself, trying to chase away the melancholy that the rainy day seems to have amplified.

While scrolling through the list of unread emails, her gaze falls on a familiar name, Axel, a dear friend and university classmate, with whom she shared not only his years of study but also his first work experiences in Europe. A smile touches her lips as she remembers the adventures they had together, a stark contrast to the loneliness of her recent days.

She opens the email with a mixture of curiosity and nostalgia. Axel, with his usual contagious enthusiasm, writes about a virtual gallery that is enjoying considerable success among art enthusiasts.

"Hi Avery, I hope you are well. I know that recent times have been difficult for you, but I thought this news might interest you and perhaps bring you a little of that joy that art always can give. In the virtual gallery of I'm talking to you, I've discovered some incredible young talents. Their works are fresh, innovative, and I think they could really catch your attention. I'll send you the link to the gallery. It would be great to hear your opinion on these emerging artists.
Big hugs , Axel."

Axel's proposal comes like a ray of sunshine on an otherwise gray day. Avery realizes how much she has missed immersing herself in the world of art, exploring new creative expressions, feeling part of the community that had once been the center of her life.
"Maybe this is exactly what I need," she thinks, feeling already lighter at the idea of discovering something new, of being surprised and inspired. With a sense of renewed curiosity, Avery clicks on the link provided by Axel, immersing herself in the world of the virtual gallery. As she explores the works of young artists, she finds herself smiling, moved by the beauty and originality of the creations she encounters. Each piece speaks to her in a different way, reawakening in her a passion for art she feared she had lost.

From creation to creation, she lets her curiosity guide her, discovering works that oscillate between the ingenious and the unusual, some so daring as to blur the line between genius and madness, others that provoke a smirk for their bold disdain for the conventional. But it is in this journey through the most eclectic contemporary art that Avery stumbles upon the creations of Jordan, a name still unknown to many but which stands out in the virtual gallery as a beacon of pure raw talent and passion.

Jordan's works are not merely images to observe; they are experiences to live. Each canvas seems to pulse with its own life, weaving intricate stories with vivid colors and bold strokes that speak directly to the soul. Avery is immediately struck by the expressive power of these pieces, by the artist's ability to explore profound themes with disarming sincerity.

"This is true talent," Avery thinks, as her gaze gets lost in a painting that seems almost to move under her eyes, telling the story of an inner struggle, of hope and despair intertwined. There is something in those brushstrokes, in the way they capture light and shadow, that makes her feel incredibly close to the artist, as if she could sense the emotions that guided his hand.

Jordan's works represent an oasis of authenticity in a sea of artistic attempts that often seem to seek shock more than true expression. Avery recognizes in him a kindred soul, an artist who, like her, believes in art as a vehicle for truth and beauty, despite the personal storms that may rage.

Intrigued and deeply moved, Avery feels a growing desire to learn more about this emerging young artist. Who is Jordan? What stories lie behind his intensely personal and touching works? And most importantly, how could she, with her experience and knowledge, help him gain the recognition he deserves?

Determined to find out more, and feeling the birth of not just admiration for artistic talent but also the seed of a possible human and professional connection that could change both of their lives, she decides to initiate a private conversation with Jordan.

Creative Convergences

"Good morning, Jordan. I'm Avery, an art critic. I had the pleasure of admiring your works at today's virtual exhibition. I must say that I was deeply impressed by your ability to capture such intense emotions with such an economy of strokes. There is one particular piece, 'Inner Resonances,' that truly captivated me. Could we talk about your art?"

Jordan, surprised and a bit incredulous to receive attention from such a renowned name in the art world, responds enthusiastically but also with a hint of nervousness:

"Hello Avery, it's an honor for me. I never imagined that my works could attract the attention of someone of your stature. 'Inner Resonances' is one of my favorites, an attempt to explore the dialogue between our inner world and the external universe. I would be happy to discuss it with you."

"Your description of the piece reveals a depth of thought that goes well beyond your age. I would like to delve deeper into understanding your creative process. And, if you're interested, I could help you expose your work to a broader audience. I have some contacts in the art world who would be excited to discover a talent like yours."

"I really don't know what to say, Avery. It would be a dream come true. My biggest challenge so far has been reaching a wider audience. Any advice or support from you would be incredibly valuable to me."

"Well, why don't we start with a review of your works on my blog? From there, we could organize an interview or a virtual presentation to introduce your work to gallery owners and collectors. I firmly believe in your potential, Jordan, and I think the art world is ready to discover your unique voice."

"It would be an incredible honor, Avery. Thank you so much for this opportunity. I'm ready to get involved and learn everything I can from this experience. Your confidence in my work motivates me to push beyond my limits."

"It's my pleasure, Jordan. And remember, every great artist started somewhere. Your journey seems to have already started on the right foot. Let's organize for a more detailed chat in the coming days. I'll send you an email with all the details."

"I look forward to it, Avery. Thanks again for this incredible opportunity. See you soon."

This exchange marks the beginning of a promising collaboration and the opening of new doors for Jordan in the art world, all thanks to Avery's expert eye and generosity.

Still immersed in the emotional reverberations left by Jordan's works, she realizes that her curiosity extends well beyond professional admiration. Merely analyzing technique or composition is no longer sufficient; she wants to understand the man behind the artist, his inspirations, his passions, his struggles. She is convinced that to truly support Jordan and perhaps spark a meaningful collaboration, establishing a personal connection, free from bias and preconceived expectations, is essential.

With this idea in mind, Avery decides to take action.

"I need to write him a new message right away," she thinks, reflecting on how to approach. She wants her interest to be clear: it's not just the hunt for new talent for her portfolio, but a genuine desire for dialogue and creative exchange.

Avery pauses for a moment, carefully pondering her words. She wants her communication to convey respect and sincere interest, without seeming intrusive or overly formal.

"Dear Jordan,

As I mentioned before, I was deeply impressed by your works in the virtual gallery. There is a truth and a beauty in your creations that speak directly to the soul, and I would be honored to learn more not only about the artist but also the person behind these powerful works.

I firmly believe that art is a dialogue, not just between the artist and their audience, but also among creators who share a similar view of the world. It would be a real pleasure for me to explore the possibility of collaboration or simply to exchange ideas and perspectives.

If you are open to this dialogue, I would be happy to organize a meeting, virtual or in person, as you prefer. I believe that together we could discover unexpected affinities and opportunities.

With sincere appreciation,

Avery"

After sending the message, Avery feels animated by a sense of hope.

"Maybe this is the beginning of something special," she tells herself, letting the enthusiasm for the potential of this new connection warm her spirit.

"My decision to seek a personal connection with Jordan stems from a deep belief that art is, first and foremost, an expression of being human. There's in me a desire to build bridges, to find that common spark that can give life to authentic collaborations capable of changing the course of things. In this search, I realize that I am not just trying to discover hidden talent, but also to rediscover parts of myself through the art of another," Avery said on the phone to Axel.

As the sound of rain continues to beat against the windows of her penthouse, Avery holds the phone tightly to her ear, listening to Axel's concerned words.

"You have to be careful, Avery," he tells her seriously.

"At this moment, you are too vulnerable. It's easy to get attached or to idealize someone like Jordan, especially when art touches you so deeply."

Avery walks slowly back and forth in the room, reflecting on her friend's words. She knows Axel is right; the wounds from her recent past have not yet fully healed, making her more susceptible to emotional impulses. Yet, something deep inside her strongly believes that this contact with Jordan could be different, a positive turning point.

"I understand, Axel, and I truly appreciate your concern," Avery responds with a calm and measured voice.
"But I assure you that I'll be cautious. This will only be a virtual contact. We'll communicate online, without risks. There's no room for getting too attached or creating false idealizations. It's just a professional and creative opportunity, nothing more."
There's a pause on the other end of the line, and Avery can almost imagine Axel nodding reluctantly.
"Alright, Avery. I trust your judgment," he finally says.
"But please, remember to protect your heart. Art can be a wonderful connection between souls, but it can also make you incredibly exposed."

Avery smiles, feeling grateful for the friend who always has her best interests at heart.
"Thank you, Axel. I'll keep your words in mind. I promise I'll proceed with caution."
After hanging up, Avery feels reassured by the conversation. Even though the path ahead is uncertain, she knows that the adventure she's about to embark on with Jordan is a conscious choice. She's determined to maintain a balance between emotional openness and protecting her own well-being, ready to explore the potential of this new virtual connection with open eyes and a cautious heart.

Virtual Openings: The Avery and Jordan Connection

Jordan is sitting in front of his computer, his gaze fixed on the screen where Avery's email is still open. Within the walls of his small loft, which seem to gather and amplify the emotions of the moment, he allows himself a mix of pride and disbelief. He can't believe what he has just read.

"This could really be the start of everything," he thinks, a smile beginning to form on his lips as his heart beats a little faster.

For Jordan, Avery's message is much more than a simple email. It's the validation of his sleepless nights spent painting, of his days filled with self-doubt and questioning his choices. It's a sign that perhaps, finally, his dream of becoming known in the art world might become reality.

"I could really make it," he tells himself, allowing himself to savor the possibility of success, to prove to all those who underestimated him that he has found his path, that he can stand out thanks to his talent and determination.

The idea of becoming famous, of seeing his name associated with artists he has always admired, gives him a surge of adrenaline.

"It would be a real moral slap for everyone who didn't believe in me," he reflects, thinking of the friends who mocked him, the acquaintances who doubted his choices, and most of all his parents.

His parents... Jordan loses himself in that thought. Their reaction to his life choice, far from conventions and family expectations, had created a deep rift. "Maybe, seeing that I can be successful, that my art is recognized, they will change their minds. Maybe they will welcome me back with open arms," he dreams, imagining a reconciliation that would heal old wounds.

But for now, what matters is the door that is opening in front of him thanks to Avery. Jordan knows this could be his chance to change everything, to transform his life and career. With new determination, he decides to respond to Avery's email, promptly but with care, knowing that this exchange could give rise to the future he has always desired.

As Jordan's fingers dance on the keyboard, a part of him wonders why he feels so comfortable opening up to Avery, a person he knows only through a screen. Yet, the sincerity and depth conveyed by her email have touched something in him, prompting him to share pieces of his life he rarely dared to explore with others.

"Dear Avery,

I cannot express how much your email has touched me. Receiving recognition and interest from a professional of your caliber is something that exceeds all my expectations. Thank you, truly, for seeing something in my works that is worth exploring further.

I find myself at a point in my life where personal and professional redemption seem to intertwine. My journey in art has always been driven by passion, but also by the search for a place in the world that I could truly call my own. Growing up, this quest often put me at odds with the expectations of those around me, especially my parents.

Sharing this with you, Avery, makes me feel strangely comfortable, as if somehow I know that you can understand. Perhaps because, through your words, I sensed an echo of that same search for authenticity and meaning that has guided my hand on every canvas.

The prospect of collaborating with you, or even just exchanging ideas, fills me with hope. Not only for the potential doors it could open in the art world, but also for the chance to redeem myself in the eyes of those who, until now, have seen my choice as a failure. Your confidence and interest in me are an incredible source of motivation to prove, perhaps first and foremost to myself, that the path I have taken is the right one.

I hope this is the beginning of an open and enriching dialogue between us, and I look forward to discovering where it can lead us.

With gratitude,
Jordan

After hitting "send," Jordan feels both vulnerable and liberated. Sharing his dreams and insecurities with Avery, a perfect stranger, feels like a bold but necessary step. After all, art is communication, and what is more artistic than opening up completely to another soul, even through the coldness of a screen?

Beep... beep... beep... Avery's alarm clock rings relentlessly at 6:40 in the morning. "Nooo," she sighs to herself, burying her face in the pillow for a few more moments. "I can't get up this morning... I might just call the office and say I'm working from home."

With a mix of reluctance and resolve, she pulls herself up, reaches for the phone, and dials Tessa, her friend and all-around secretary, who has always been able to expertly handle emergencies and unforeseen events.

"Hi Tessa, I'm not feeling the best today, I think I'll work from home. Could you take care of the urgent matters at the office and update me via email or phone for the rest?"

Tessa, always understanding and efficient, accepts without hesitation, assuring Avery that everything will be handled in the best way. "Don't worry, Avery. Rest and focus on what you need to do. I'll keep you updated on everything."

Reassured, Avery heads to the kitchen to prepare a simple but comforting toast and coffee, essential for dispelling the remnants of sleep and starting the day. As the coffee slowly brews, her thoughts turn to the upcoming opening exhibition for the inauguration of the new business center, a project that is particularly close to her heart.

"I need to create something memorable, something that leaves a mark," Avery reflects, sipping her coffee.

"It will be an excellent opportunity to highlight emerging artists like Jordan, offering them a significant showcase." The idea of contributing to the success of yet unrecognized talents excites her, fueling her determination to overcome tiredness and turn this day into a productive opportunity.

Between bites of toast and sips of coffee, Avery begins to mentally outline the layout of the exhibition, thinking about how to arrange the works to maximize the visual and emotional impact on the guests.

"I also need to talk with the design team and the marketing department to ensure that the event's communication meets expectations," she reminds herself, mentally noting the key points to discuss.

Avery's day, which started with the temptation to stay under the covers, transforms into a whirlwind of creativity and planning. Despite the tiredness, the thought of significantly contributing to the careers of artists like Jordan and the opening of the new business center gives her the energy needed to face the challenges ahead. Back in front of her PC, she sees that Jordan has responded to her email...

Beyond Art: Sharing and Connections

" Dear Avery,

In my previous email, I mentioned the rift between me and my parents without going into details. I think it's important, for our budding connection, that you also know this part of me. My detachment from the family didn't arise solely from my choice to pursue the path of art but was also deeply influenced by a relationship I had with Ethan, a guy my age who I met during my university years. Ethan was the opposite of me in almost everything. Extroverted, sunny, a lover of life and travel, he felt like a citizen of the world. His energy and desire to explore every corner of the planet fascinated me; he was like a shooting star that lit up everything in its path. I, on the other hand, was more introverted and introspective, rarely stepping out of my comfort zone, and found it difficult to open up to others. My art was my refuge, the only place where I truly felt comfortable. My relationship with Ethan was a real whirlwind in my life, an experience that shook my foundations and made me see the world from a completely different perspective. With him, I learned to look beyond the confines of my art studio, to dream of travels and adventures in places I could only imagine before.

However, when my parents found out about our relationship, they didn't take it well. They couldn't understand, or perhaps didn't want to accept, the nature of our bond. The tension created by this situation led to frequent arguments, until I decided it was better for me to distance myself, both physically and emotionally, from what had become a stifling environment.

Sharing all this with you, Avery, makes me incredibly vulnerable, but strangely I don't feel uncomfortable. I feel that, somehow, you might understand and accept this part of me without judgment. My hope, in starting this dialogue with you, is not only to find professional collaboration but also to build a human connection based on sincerity and mutual understanding.

Thank you for listening to me and for being, even through a screen, a welcoming presence in my life.

With affection,
Jordan"

Sending this email, Jordan feels as though he has let go of some of the weight he carried inside. The possibility of being understood and accepted for who he is, without masks or pretense, gives him a sense of hope that he hadn't felt in a long time.

"With affection?" Avery muses on these words as she re-reads Jordan's email. It had been a long time since she received a message so full of sincerity, except perhaps from Axel, her always reliable touchstone. In the digital age, we are so used to communicating with quick exchanges and expressive icons - winks, virtual kisses, digital hugs - that the weight of true words seems almost forgotten.
"But what remains authentic, after all this?" she wonders, with a hint of skepticism.

Perhaps, Avery reflects, her tendency to scrutinize every word, to search for the hidden meaning behind each sentence, makes her overly critical. Yet, she can't help but think that every word, every chosen symbol, carries a deep meaning, an essence that, if not used with care and awareness, risks fading away, depriving communication of that rare and precious potential for human connection.

> "Every 'with affection' should be a promise, a connection between souls," muses Avery, "not just a simple farewell or a circumstantial closure." Jordan's email, with its genuine expression of gratitude and openness, reminds her that, despite the cynicism that sometimes assails her, there are still those who choose their words with the heart, who are not afraid to show affection, even through the cold screen of a computer.

Reflecting on Jordan's email, Avery realizes how much she wants to delve deeper into the life of this intriguing artist. Beyond art, what drives his life? What are the little things that make him unique? With a mix of curiosity and anticipation, she decides to send a new email, hoping to invite Jordan to share more about himself, about what excites him beyond the canvas.

"Dear Jordan,

Your last email was a true pleasure to read. It made me reflect on how art can be a bond between people, even when they are far apart. But it also made me curious to learn more about you, the man behind the artist. Besides art, what are you passionate about? What are your musical tastes? Are there any films or novels that have touched you particularly, that you hold dear to your heart?

In continuing her email to Jordan, Avery finds herself navigating the delicate waters of personal curiosity. She wants to know more about how Jordan manages his daily life, especially in financial terms, given that the path of an artist can be rugged and uncertain until a certain recognition is achieved. However, she is aware of not wanting to turn her interest into an interrogation, aiming to keep the conversation light and respectful.
In formulating her words, she decides to include this reflection in her message, hoping to communicate her sincerity and the desire for reciprocity in sharing personal experiences.
And she adds:

"Jordan, if I may ask a somewhat more personal question, I was wondering how you manage the day-to-day, considering the challenges that we artists often face, especially at the beginning of our careers. I hope it doesn't seem too intrusive; it's just that, having shared so much of yourself, I feel that this part of your life is also a piece of the mosaic you are creating. Of course, only if you feel comfortable sharing it.

And to keep our exchange balanced, I promise I will also open up more about myself. I believe there is immense value in sharing our stories, not just the joys but also the challenges, because that's how we can truly connect as people, beyond our artworks."

Avery hopes that this open and honest approach will encourage Jordan to feel free to share the details of his life without feeling pressured. She wants him to know that her interest comes from a desire to understand and support, not to judge. It's an attempt to weave a deeper bond, founded on mutual respect and sharing of experiences, in the hope that this dialogue can enrich them both.

"I am always looking for new inspirations and firmly believe that the people we meet, the stories we share, can enrich us as much as a work of art. I hope you don't mind my curiosity. I would love to hear your stories and share mine, in a dialogue that can go beyond art, touching the nuances that make up our lives.

With affection,
Avery"

Pressing "send," Avery feels as though she has opened a small window into her world, inviting Jordan to do the same. It's an act of trust, an extension of the hand across the vast digital space, hoping to find an echo, a smile, a response that could bring them closer together.

Cold Outside, Warmth Inside

Outside, the cold is biting: the thermometer shows -5 degrees, but the gusts of icy wind make it feel much colder, almost -15 degrees Celsius. Jordan, who has never obtained a driver's license, finds himself having to rely on public transportation or walking around the city. Despite the efficiency of the transport system, waiting even just five minutes at the bus stop in these weather conditions becomes a real test of endurance.

He has never liked the harsh climate. The possibility of working from home is a salvation, but for all other daily needs, Jordan is forced to go outside. There was a time, right after his relationship with Ethan ended, when he opted to order groceries online, completely isolating himself from the outside world for weeks. However, that choice had a negative impact on his psycho-physical well-being, forcing him to impose on himself to go out at least once a week, if only to do the shopping.

Not that things have improved much since then. In the three years he has spent in that city, Jordan has not been able to make friends. People, although friendly and ready to help when needed, tend to retreat into their own world as soon as possible, showing little inclination for empathy. Thinking he could break this isolation, Jordan had also tried joining a gym, despite his aversion to physical activity, hoping to meet new people. The experiment, however, lasted less than three months: even there, exchanges were limited to a formal "good morning," making the environment unsuitable for fostering new friendships.

The feeling of isolation intensifies in the shopping centers of the city, where Jordan has noticed an almost surreal atmosphere. Despite the presence of many people, an unusual silence prevails, as if almost everyone were speaking in whispers or, more simply, not speaking at all. Even the automatic checkout machines, with their mechanical beeps, seem to emit muffled sounds, as if they were equipped with silencers. This strange quietness, instead of comforting him, amplifies the sense of alienation that Jordan feels living in this place, far from the warm bustle he was used to.

Avery types with frustration on her cell phone: "Why are you ignoring my messages? I don't care what you're doing or who you're with, I just want to know when you will come to pick up your things." Her mind silently adds: "Irresponsible..."

The presence of Eric's boxes, cluttering the studio for over five months and turning it into a dusty storage space, forces her to move her work to the living room. Their relationship had begun fifteen years ago, bringing with it a whirlwind of emotions: overwhelming, passionate, and full of happy moments. Eric, a criminal lawyer of great seriousness and competence, became an extroverted and carefree man outside the courtroom, perhaps too much so, Avery reflects in hindsight. From the beginning of their story, she had plunged into the world of art, timidly exhibiting at the first shows in her hometown, then expanding in Europe thanks to the contagious enthusiasm of Axel, her steadfast support, who had helped her achieve success after years of hard work.

While continuing to paint occasionally, Avery had discovered her vocation in supporting aspiring young artists, helping them navigate the complex universe of contemporary art. Now an established art critic, she considered the Museum of Modern Art (MoMA) in New York almost a second home. The MoMA, located at 11 West 53rd Street, between Fifth Avenue and Sixth Avenue, has been a fundamental catalyst for the spread of Modern Art internationally, earning a reputation as one of the most influential museum centers in the world. Its collection, a broad anthology that ranges from architecture to photography, from screen printing to design, and to multimedia art, in addition to classic paintings and sculptures, covers a timeline from the late 19th century to the present, witnessing the evolution of modern and contemporary art.

Returning home after running daily errands, including grocery shopping, paying some bills, and picking up laundry at the automatic laundromat, Jordan dedicates himself to cooking with the same creative spirit he applies to his art. A lover of intense flavors, he enjoys experimenting with spices and has a soft spot for sushi and vegetables. Today he decides to prepare curry basmati rice, which he sometimes cooks with pieces of chicken, other times preferring an exclusively vegetarian version.

On days when culinary inspiration is lacking, Jordan doesn't mind indulging in some guilty pleasures like burgers and fries, a small tribute to the joy of simpler and immediate food.

However, his real talent in the kitchen shines in pastry making, especially in preparing sweet potato pie, his specialty. This delicacy consists of a crumbly shortcrust pastry shell enveloping a soft and sweet heart of sweet potato puree, enriched with a mix of spices and orange zest for a distinctive aroma. This dessert, in its apparent simplicity, is an explosion of flavors that tells stories of tradition and family affection.

The recipe was passed down to him by his beloved grandmother Lynette, whose American roots introduced Jordan to sweet potato pie as an essential element of Thanksgiving Day celebrations. For Jordan, this pie is not just a dessert, but a connection to his origins and the happy memories spent in the kitchen beside his grandmother, learning the secrets of a dish that is much more than a simple recipe: it's a piece of family history, a memory of love that endures over time.

Sitting in front of his aromatic plate of rice, Jordan can't help but let his thoughts drift toward Avery. Despite not knowing what she looks like, something inside him starts to stir, a new and exciting feeling. There's something special brewing between them, something he can't precisely define, but of which he's certain: the loneliness that has characterized his life until now seems destined to fade.

After finishing his meal, Jordan approaches the computer, driven by the hope of finding a new message from Avery. And his expectations are met.

"She would really like to hear my stories and share hers..." he reflects, a glimmer of doubt crossing his mind. "Maybe I was too impetuous in telling her about myself. But now I want to find out if her interest in my life is genuine; I'll ask her to tell me something about herself."

With this intention, Jordan begins to compose a new message, searching for the right words to invite Avery to share parts of her life. He wants this exchange to go beyond mere professional curiosity, aspiring to create a deeper bond based on reciprocity and sincerity.

"Dearest Avery,

I was truly happy to read your last message and to feel your desire to share stories and experiences. I think this is what makes our conversations so valuable: the opportunity to go beyond mere words and to touch each other's lives with authenticity and warmth.

Now, if you don't mind, I would really like to know more about you. What are the passions that animate your life outside the world of art? Is there a particular memory, a moment, or an experience that you feel has shaped the person you are today?

I eagerly await hearing your stories, hoping that our exchange can continue to grow and enrich us both.

With sincere affection,
Jordan"

Pressing "send," Jordan feels a mix of trepidation and excitement. With each message, each exchange, he grows closer to Avery, exploring together an uncharted territory that promises to be rich with discoveries.

He has immersed himself in this relationship with a fervor that betrays his desire to escape the monotony of reality, seeking in Avery both a refuge and a source of inspiration. This deep longing for connection and understanding is reminiscent of the first sentimental explorations of adolescence.

Between Art and Virtual Connections

"Thank you for the update, Tessa. When you have a moment, could you get in touch with the organizer of the vernissage? I think I have found the ideal artist for the event..." With these words, Avery ends the call, her mind already projecting towards the upcoming exhibition. "I will undoubtedly invite Jordan to exhibit 'Inner Resonances'. I am convinced that it will be the piece to launch him into the pantheon of art," she reflects, animated by a mix of enthusiasm and determination.
"Oh, I almost forgot, I have a business lunch today, and then I need to meet Lorraine..." she remembers, almost surprised by her own distraction, as she hurries to get into the shower.

The lunch takes place at Il Gattopardo, a renowned Italian restaurant in the heart of Manhattan, famous for the excellence of its dishes and impeccable service. Its pasta dishes are particularly praised, often considered by many to be the best Italian restaurant in New York, and the selection of wines is simply exceptional.

Avery has a soft spot for Italian cuisine, a love born during her six months in Florence, during her European adventure. There, she learned to love the classics of Tuscan cuisine: from pasta to hearty dishes like bistecca alla fiorentina, to ribollita, and sweet delights like zuccotto fiorentino.
The latter, in particular, encapsulates a fascinating story linked to the late Renaissance, when the Medici dominated the European scene.

Caterina de' Medici, who became the Queen of France, commissioned Bernardo Buontalenti, the inventor of gelato, to create an unprecedented dessert to celebrate the arrival of Spanish ambassadors. Thus, the zuccotto was born, initially called "Caterina's Helmet", thought to have been prepared inside a military helmet of the time. The original version of the dessert was significantly different from the modern one, being made of ricotta, cocoa nibs, citrus candied fruits, wrapped in a sponge cake soaked in Alchermes, giving the dessert an intense bright red color. Over time, zuccotto underwent variations, including cream among the ingredients but maintaining its historical and gastronomic charm.

Every business lunch at Il Gattopardo turns into a triumph, and for Avery, who is not prone to superstitions, has chosen this restaurant as her preferred place for every initial professional meeting. By now, the staff recognizes her and greets her with familiarity, making her feel almost as if she were at home. However, that day Avery finds herself unusually distracted. A notification on her cell phone reveals the arrival of a new email from Jordan, but she decides to resist the temptation to open it right there, surrounded by people she does not know. She wants to save that moment for when she will be in the comfort of her home, in an intimate and personal environment, almost as if to jealously guard the first steps of this budding relationship away from outside eyes.

As soon as she finds a moment to pause, Avery hurries to take her leave, feeling the pressing need to retreat to her personal space. She tries to contact Lorraine for an appointment they had, but after a few rings, the recorded voice of the answering machine informs her that her friend cannot answer. Without wasting time, Avery leaves a message: "Dear, I know we had planned to meet, I am really sorry but an unexpected emergency forces me to move to another part of the city. I promise that I will call you back to arrange a new meeting next week!"

With her mind already projected towards home, Avery feels the impatience to return to her refuge, her nest, where she can finally indulge in the luxury of opening and peacefully savoring Jordan's new message, enveloped in the warmth and privacy of her four walls. The idea of being able to read Jordan's words unhurriedly, in a familiar and reassuring environment, fills her with a sweet and somewhat anxious anticipation, a clear sign of how much this budding connection has already begun to mean to her.

Finally sitting in front of her computer, Avery has shed the formalities of her ivory suit; her high-heeled shoes lie haphazardly on the carpet, a small act of rebellion against the rigidity of the day just passed.
Avery has embraced this new adventure with an almost childlike curiosity, allowing herself to dream and hope for possibilities that everyday life had made her forget. Her attitude is a blend of innocence and unconditional hope in the transformative power of love and friendship.

With a mix of trepidation and excitement, she clicks on Jordan's email and begins to read.

His words challenge her: "What are the passions that animate your life outside the world of art? Is there a particular memory, a moment, or an experience that you feel has shaped the person you are today?" Avery can't help but smile thoughtfully: "I should have expected this from Jordan... after all, it was I who suggested this honest exchange."
And so, Avery begins to unravel the threads of her life, typing at a steady pace. She talks about a marriage that was initially happy, lived with passion and complicity for the first six years, before the shadows of betrayal began to creep into their relationship. The most painful memory is related to Eric, her ex-husband, and his affair with a 19-year-old intern. Avery recalls with bitterness how Eric had introduced the young woman into their lives, presenting her as his secretary and driver, a necessity dictated by the suspension of his license after failing a breathalyzer test.

The decision to share these intimate and painful details is not easy for Avery, but she feels that this exchange of truth with Jordan is an important step.

"If we really want to get to know each other," she thinks, "we must be willing to show even the most fragile parts of ourselves." With this conviction, Avery opens up completely, entrusting Jordan not only with the highlights but also the shadows of her past, in the hope that this mutual sincerity can lay the groundwork for a deep and authentic connection.

"As for the person I am today, I don't think I have heroic stories to tell: I've always played by the rules, never sought to stand out or challenge the status quo, I've adapted to what the system demanded without too much resistance. I've never known true poverty or need, having grown up in a family that, although not extremely wealthy, never let me want for anything. My childhood was peaceful and full of love, enriched by travel, gifts, and attention, benefits due to being an only child.

It was in adulthood that I began to face real challenges. Entering a work environment dominated by a male culture and, in some ways, misogynistic, forced me to work twice as hard to gain the recognition I deserved. However, I have proven that, in the end, competence outweighs any gender bias. I find the debate on gender quotas almost amusing: if you are not competent, your sex will not magically make you suitable for a certain role. There are no gendered ideas, there are just ideas.

I hope these lines answer your curiosities. At the moment, if I think about my passions beyond art, I realize I don't have much to say. I am going through a phase of life where I feel a kind of inner void, which I hope to fill in the near future. However, there is something I am absolutely certain of: writing to you is a moment of deep reflection for me, almost cathartic. I eagerly await the time when I can sit down and let the words flow freely, helping me to organize my thoughts, in the belief that you will be able to grasp their deepest meaning.

Thank you, Jordan, for the trust you have shown in me. I wish for our exchange of messages to continue to be a daily appointment for us, an opportunity to build our exclusive space together, a virtual place where no one else can enter. A corner of the world all our own, where we can express ourselves freely and share our existence in a genuine and sincere way.

Avery"

Avery is a mature woman, embodying in her daily life the wisdom and balance that only years and lived experiences can provide. Hers is a reassuring presence, her words are considered, and her actions are always measured, the result of a long series of lessons learned, sometimes at a high price, along the journey of life. However, beneath this surface of maturity and composure, there still dwells that curious, impulsive, and sometimes irrationally optimistic girl she once was.

This eternal youth within her makes its way into Avery's decisions, especially when it comes to matters of the heart and passions. It's the voice that pushes her to venture into the virtual world in search of new connections, despite the caution her age would advise. It's the spark of enthusiasm in her eyes when she talks about art, new projects, or when she imagines possibilities that many would consider unrealistic or out of reach.

The girl inside Avery makes her vulnerable but, at the same time, gives her incredible strength and the ability to see the world with ever-new eyes, to wonder and dream without limits.

This dual nature creates a fascinating contrast in Avery: on one hand, the woman who knows how to be in the world, who understands the value of time and moves with caution; on the other, the young girl who lets herself be carried away by emotions, who believes in the impossible and always seeks the magic in life.

This dualism is evident in her approach to the relationship with Jordan. While the mature woman in her carefully evaluates the implications of a bond born in such an unusual context, weighing risks and potential disappointments, the inner girl gets involved without reservation, driven by the desire to explore, to know, and perhaps to love unconditionally.

In Avery, therefore, caution and surrender coexist, reflection and impulsiveness, in a balance that is always precarious but incredibly vital. It's this amalgamation that makes her life rich and complex, and her story with Jordan a journey of continuous discovery, not only of the other but, above all, of herself.

"Now I can finally say that my day has come to an end."
"You've handled everything very well, Avery," she tells herself, as she carefully removes her makeup and prepares for the night. Even before the alarm rings, she is already awake, ready to discuss the week's commitments with Tessa. She has scheduled a new meeting with Lorraine and feels recharged with an energy that had been missing in recent months.
Then she remembers Axel.
"Oh my, his message had escaped my attention," she thinks, opening the messaging app to read what he wrote:

"Hi Avery, all good? Lorraine told me you couldn't meet... I hope you haven't changed your mind! If you have a free moment in the next few days, how about we meet for a drink? It's been too long since last time and, frankly, messages aren't enough for me anymore. I'd love for us to catch up and chat, maybe over a nice glass of red wine, like old times. Let me know when you can. A kiss."

Reading these words, Avery realizes how much she values Axel's company.
"I absolutely must find time for him," she reflects, with a smile. The prospect of spending time with such a dear friend, sharing laughs and memories, warms her heart. Avery is determined to make room in her schedule for Axel, aware of how precious his friendship is and eager to renew those moments of sharing that have always enriched her life.

Recently, Jordan's career as a freelance illustrator has taken a positive turn, with an increase in projects and an improvement in his financial situation. This successful period, combined with the promise of greater visibility for his work, seems to mark the beginning of a more promising phase in his life. However, it's the encounter with Avery that represents the real turning point. Avery's proposal to maintain daily contact has filled Jordan with joy, turning into a moment both eagerly anticipate.

"Dearest Avery,

I fully share your enthusiasm for our daily exchanges, which have become indispensable. Your presence has made my days lighter and full of happiness, for which I am deeply grateful. I feel a strong connection between us, a bond that I believe can only grow stronger and hold pleasant surprises. It might surprise you, but every time I sit down to write to you, I feel a unique emotion, almost as if you were here with me, in a way I struggle to express in words.

If you read this message tonight, I wish you a peaceful good night; if you read it tomorrow, I hope your day will be wonderful.

Sending you a hug and looking forward to hearing from you again.
Jordan"

After reading Jordan's words, Avery finds herself wrapped in a sleepless night, but it's a new, exhilarating kind of insomnia that makes her feel as if she's living her first date. The feelings stirring in her, evoked by metaphors like "having butterflies in the stomach," "love at first sight," or "love is blind," are grounded not only in the poetry of love but also in the science behind it.

These tumultuous emotions and the physical symptoms that accompany them, such as an accelerated heartbeat or a certain nervousness, result from precise chemical reactions orchestrated by her brain. At the heart of this emotional whirlwind are neurotransmitters like dopamine and noradrenaline, the chemical messengers that trigger in Avery a sense of happiness and well-being, typical of falling in love.

These same compounds, responsible for the euphoria now engulfing Avery, are not exclusive to romantic feelings but are involved in various gratifying experiences of life, from appreciating a delicious meal to fulfilling a deep desire.

Thus, as the night hours relentlessly unfold, Avery finds herself navigating this sea of sensations, recognizing that what she is experiencing with Jordan is a complex amalgam of science and poetry, an intertwining of brain mechanisms and pure emotional magic. It's a falling in love that transcends mere attraction, since they have never met, enriched by an emotion that makes its way through the daily chaos to reveal itself in all its power, uniting two hearts with the precision of a chemical equation.

As Avery leaves her penthouse, taking the elevator that opens directly into her apartment, she thinks of the blog.
"I need to write that post about Jordan's works," she reflects, a thought accompanying her as she walks out the door.

The day seems unusually bright; the city streets sparkle with new light, the people she meets seem to smile more easily, and a fresh, unknown aroma wafts through the air. This sense of novelty and liveliness follows her as she drives to the office, immersing her in a positive and contemplative mood.

Arriving at work, Avery greets Tessa with warmth that goes beyond the usual professional courtesy.
"Hi Tessa, how are you? I hope all is well...that dress looks great on you," she says, pouring herself another coffee. Tessa is almost astonished; Avery has always been a figure of respect and professionalism, an admirable leader, but she had never ventured beyond the work sphere to enter the personal realm of her colleagues. This change, though unexpected, fills her with joy. Seeing Avery so serene and open is a novelty that hadn't been recorded for a long time, and this touch of humanity adds a special light to the workday.

From the Bounds of Illustration: Discovering Jordan

In an era where contemporary art continues to explore new expressive dimensions, artists emerge whose work reflects a unique and deeply personal vision. Today, on our contemporary art blog, I want to introduce you to an extraordinary talent who is capturing the attention of critics and art enthusiasts with his vibrant and emotionally charged paintings: Jordan.

Having started his career as a freelance illustrator, with projects ranging from digital publishing to web graphics, Jordan has evolved his passion into a vocation for painting. This transition has marked the beginning of a new and promising phase in his artistic life. His canvases, expressions of bold colors and deep emotional themes, are tangible proof of his ability to transform the blank canvas into an intense visual narrative, capable of capturing the complexity of human emotions with decisive strokes and a rich and varied color palette.

Jordan demonstrates that, even in an era dominated by digital art, painting retains a unique power of emotional connection and non-verbal communication. Each work he creates is a dialogue between the artist and the viewer, an invitation to explore stories told through the universal language of shapes and colors.

But what distinguishes Jordan is not just the intrinsic quality of his work; it is also his ability to establish an emotional bond with those who view his pieces. As an art critic, I have had the opportunity to immerse myself in his portfolio and can attest that each piece is an open window to the artist's soul, offering a visual experience that is both personal and universal.

At this crucial moment in his career, Jordan is ready to emerge from anonymity, establishing himself as a significant voice in the contemporary art scene. His collaboration with me represents just the beginning of an exciting journey that promises to bring his works in front of a broader audience and earn the attention and recognition he deserves.

I invite collectors, art enthusiasts, and the simply curious to discover Jordan's painterly world. In his works, you will find not only a source of inspiration and beauty but also an opportunity for deep emotional connection. Stay tuned for updates on his upcoming exhibitions and initiatives. Jordan's art is not just to be admired; it's an experience to be fully lived.

Avery

The phone call

"Yes, Lorraine, I admit there's a sea of issues to resolve, but these last few weeks have been really hectic for me," Avery confesses with a sigh of exhaustion.

"I understand, Avery, I know it's not easy for you to deal with this situation, but it's time to definitively close the chapter with Eric. The separation was tumultuous, marked by continuous bickering, but in the end, you reached an agreement... You shouldn't delay finalizing the divorce," insists Lorraine with a decisive tone.

Lorraine, a family law specialist and Avery's trusted friend, is known for her firmness and expertise. Nearing retirement, her reputation in court is such that many lawyers in New York, though young and ambitious, prefer not to cross her path in the courtroom. Her experience is extensive, her character indomitable, and her knowledge of the law impeccable, enriched by an infallible female intuition.

She was the only one capable of confronting Eric. During the separation, despite the obvious infidelities, Eric had attempted to defame Avery and take as much as possible from her. However, he hadn't counted on Lorraine's tenacity...

"Alright, Lorraine, let's meet at my place tonight. I'll prepare something to eat, and we can sort out all the details," Avery finally proposes. She is aware that it's the wisest decision, although every discussion about her past with Eric weighs heavily on her, feeling like a closed chapter of her life.

Avery is now fully immersed in the here and now, finding in Jordan that much-desired change. She feels that the bond uniting them is intensifying, becoming significant for both. There is also a subtle magic in their virtual communication: there's no need to dress in a particular way or to care for appearances to share thoughts and emotions, allowing her to freely live her feelings from the comfort of her living room. However, Avery aspires to greater privacy in their interactions, outside the formal context of her professional email inbox. She is determined to suggest to Jordan that they switch to a private messaging app, thus transforming their relationship from a mere work connection to a personal and intimate one.

"Dear Jordan,

Your last email touched me deeply... I won't hesitate to tell you that I spent the whole night awake, with you in my thoughts. You seem so close, despite the distance between us.

I would like to suggest something: how about we drop the emails and switch to phone numbers to communicate through a messaging app? For more personal conversations, I find it's the best solution. And, if you like, we could also take the opportunity to hear each other, maybe with a phone call. What do you think?

I care deeply about respecting your privacy and won't insist further, but it would be nice to get even closer in this way.

I eagerly await your response and send you a warm hug.

With affection,

Avery"

"Finally, Avery..." exclaims Jordan, browsing through his emails with a mix of relief and anxiety. The fear that his last message might have caused her to withdraw was palpable. Throughout the day, thoughts of her become a constant echo in his mind.

The computer screen has become his anchor, not only for work but also as a window to Avery. Even when he tries to focus on painting, the urge to check his email becomes irresistible.

"Exchanging phone numbers! I should have thought of that," he chides himself, feeling clumsy in these relational dynamics. Despite his past with Ethan, Avery wasn't the only woman to quicken his heart, but no previous relationship had ever left such a deep imprint.
"I don't know her personally," he reflects, "yet I feel incredibly connected to her."

"Dearest Avery,

Firstly, let me express my gratitude for the article you wrote on your blog. It was a magnificent gesture that I sincerely appreciate and hope to reciprocate in the future.

I fully agree with the proposal to communicate through our phones. It would be fantastic to hear your voice and interact in a more direct and personal way. Here is my number.
Regarding the messaging app, I don't use the more common ones; instead, I suggest downloading this other app, considered the most secure on the market, with end-to-end encryption for all conversations.

How about we talk tonight? Feel free to call me whenever you prefer.

Sending you a strong hug,
Jordan"

(Phone rings) "Jordan?"... "Avery? Yes, it's me, Avery. How are you?" Jordan's voice resonates with surprise and pleasure. "Wow, it's great to hear your voice," he responds, "I didn't expect you to call so quickly."

"Sorry, Jordan, did I interrupt? Tonight I invited a good friend over for dinner and was afraid of running late..."

"No, not at all, you did well to call. It's unusual, but in a wonderful way, to hear your voice," Jordan says, his tone reflecting a mix of surprise and admiration.

"Your voice is calm and reassuring, exactly how I imagined Avery would be"... "Thank you, Jordan. Your voice is also pleasant, deep and clear at the same time," Avery responds, with a hint of warmth and appreciation in her voice.

"How was your day, Jordan?"

"Really great, thanks, especially after reading your review on the blog about my works... But tell me about yourself, Avery. Who's coming to dinner at your place?"

"Tonight I've invited Lorraine, a dear friend and also my lawyer. As you know, I'm in the process of separating from Eric, and it's time to finally conclude the divorce. Like all relationships that come to an end, I look forward to turning the page and not having to talk about it anymore. In hindsight, it's easy to see things differently. For instance, I wouldn't encourage a couple to get married anymore; it seems that everything today is more ephemeral, people unite and separate too easily... Sorry, I sound a bit pessimistic. What do you think?"

Jordan listens carefully, reflecting for a moment before responding.

"I understand what you mean, Avery. It's true, relationships today seem to follow different rhythms compared to the past, quicker and perhaps more fickle. But I don't think you're being defeatist; you're just being realistic, given what you've experienced. As for marriage or any form of union, I believe it depends a lot on the individuals involved. Some find in marriage a sense of security and belonging, while others may feel freer without it. I think the key is understanding what works best for oneself, without being too influenced by conventions or others' expectations. And, speaking of taking and leaving, I believe every experience, good or bad, teaches us something important about ourselves and what we truly want from life. So, even if it may seem like a difficult time, it could also be an opportunity to grow and discover new possibilities."

Avery is surprised by Jordan's thorough and mature response. She did not expect such a reflective and understanding analysis on such a complex subject. Her surprise mixes with growing admiration for him, recognizing how Jordan is able to look beyond the surface of situations, offering a balanced and sensible perspective. This conversation adds a new layer to their connection, making her appreciate even more the depth of his thought and his ability to express complex concepts with clarity and empathy. Avery realizes that Jordan is not only a talented artist but also a person with great emotional intelligence, a quality that makes her feel even closer to him.

New hopes and shadows of the past

"The doorbell rings, signaling that Lorraine has arrived. Avery, seizing the moment, ends the call with Jordan, promising to resume their conversation the next day. "Thank you, Jordan, for the pleasant chat. I wish you a peaceful night, see you tomorrow." "See you tomorrow, Avery, take care."

As she enters, Lorraine immediately notices an unusual sparkle in Avery's eyes.
"Come on, tell me everything. What's new? It's obvious from a mile away that you have something on your mind," she presses, curious to discover the reason for such enthusiasm.

"Alright, Lorraine, but first take off your coat..." Avery begins, inviting her to make the moment more confidential. "Remember my friend Axel? He's also in the art world and recently introduced me to some emerging artists. Well, one in particular has caught my attention with his creations, so much so that we've started corresponding. The more we message, the more I feel a strong connection between us. This exchange is becoming really special to me; it makes me feel good. Just before you arrived, we had our first real phone call. You can't imagine the thrill of hearing his voice for the first time..."

"So, who is this lucky guy? What's his name? Where does he live? What does he do? How old is he?" Lorraine interrogates with a tone reminiscent of a courtroom.
"Hey, Lorraine, slow down a bit, we're not in court," Avery responds with a smile, trying to lighten the mood.

"I'll tell you everything, but let's do it over a good glass of Merlot. It's still your favorite, right?"

"Of course, you know me too well," replies Lorraine, softening her tone.

"Well, his name is Jordan. He's a web illustrator and an exceptional talent in painting. And despite his young age, he shows surprising maturity," shares Avery. "Wait, Avery, are you telling me you don't know where he lives, how he lives, or even how old he is?" Lorraine asks, visibly surprised.
"And what exactly do you mean by 'mature for his age'?"

"Well, Jordan must be quite young, given that the virtual gallery was reserved for young talents, from 18 to 28 years... I don't know exactly where he lives and, honestly, it doesn't matter to me at the moment. For now, what we have is more than enough for me," Avery responds calmly.

"Avery," Lorraine interjects, a bit worried, "this isn't like you. It almost feels like a blind date... He could be a married man, or someone looking to take advantage of your position. And does he know anything about you? Does he know how old you are, that you're getting divorced, that you live in one of the most exclusive penthouses in New York?"

Avery perceives a hint of paranoia in Lorraine's words, expressing concerns about her new "relationship" with Jordan. Despite this, Avery fervently defends this new connection she is exploring, convinced of its authenticity and the positive impact it has on her life. She emphasizes how this connection with Jordan represents a ray of light and hope, a sentiment she hadn't felt for a long time.

During the conversation, Lorraine doesn't fail to remind Avery of the importance of proceeding with the signing of the divorce papers from Eric, a crucial step to definitively close a painful chapter of her life and fully open up to new possibilities.

At the end of the evening, as Lorraine prepares to leave Avery's penthouse, with the documents finally signed, she continues to give advice to her friend. Her voice is laden with concern but also affection, as she urges Avery to proceed with caution, to protect her heart, and not to forget the lessons learned from the past.

"Be careful, Avery. It's good to see you so happy, but don't let your guard down," advises Lorraine, as she crosses the threshold, leaving Avery to reflect on her words.

While Jordan is reflecting on recent developments in his life and the emotions stirred by the conversation with Avery, his phone begins to ring. Hoping it's Avery, he answers reflexively, without even thinking to check the caller ID. However, instead of the voice he wished to hear, on the other end is Ethan, determined to engage in a conversation after three years of silence."

The surprise of hearing Ethan catches him completely off guard. Ethan's voice, once so familiar and now laden with memories, shakes Jordan's emotional stability, causing a slight tremor in his voice. This unexpected contact reveals that, despite the time passed and experiences lived, Ethan still has the ability to significantly influence him.

Jordan finds himself having to manage a tumult of conflicting emotions, disturbed by the fact that the past has knocked on his door just as he was starting to look forward with renewed optimism thanks to his growing connection with Avery.

"What do you want, Ethan? Don't make me believe you're calling just to chat... I know you, tell me the truth," Jordan insists, going on the defensive. Ethan, with his usual nonchalance, replies, "Really, I don't need anything. I'm just passing through town and thought it might be nice to meet up, maybe for a coffee..."

"You know I don't drink coffee," Jordan cuts him off, unconvinced by the invitation.
"It was just a figure of speech, come on, don't be difficult... Are you at home? Can I come over?" insists Ethan.

Jordan feels confused: the memory of the pain he felt when Ethan left is still fresh, and now that he has found a new balance and is exploring a relationship, albeit virtual, the idea of seeing him again makes him anxious. Despite everything, he can't refuse his request.
"Alright, come over, but I warn you, I only have ten minutes. I'm tired and planning to go to bed early tonight."
"I promise, just ten minutes. See you soon, Jordy," Ethan concludes, leaving Jordan to reflect on the decision he just made and the conflicting emotions this old acquaintance still manages to stir in him.

"Good morning, I hope you're well. Sorry about last night, I had to end the conversation quickly; Lorraine had already arrived. I'm heading to the office now. Call me whenever you want. A kiss, Avery," types Avery as the elevator takes her to a new day. She can hardly believe the changes in her life: the chapter with Eric is now behind her, ready only to be filed away with the deposit of the final documents, and she is getting closer to Jordan, marking the end of her loneliness.

Meanwhile, Jordan is sitting on his bed, hands in his hair, overwhelmed by a deep sense of guilt. Beside him, Ethan is still sleeping, testimony to a weakness that, once again, he failed to resist. "Here I go again. I never make the right choice," he reflects bitterly, questioning his inability to maintain a straightforward path without self-destructing.
"How can I be so vulnerable and naive? Now I'll wake him up and send him away. It's incredible how I manage to sabotage the positive moments in my life with my own hands."

Grasping his phone, he notices Avery's message. Uncertainty assails him; he doesn't know how to respond, and the idea of calling her seems out of the question. The awareness of the situation he has put himself in and the fear of the consequences on the budding relationship with Avery leave him in a state of emotional paralysis.

The secrets

Avery immerses herself in her work project all morning, but she can't shake off a sense of oddity due to Jordan's silence. She wonders if perhaps he stayed up late, absorbed in transferring some new inspiration onto canvas, and is now catching up on lost sleep. This hypothesis offers her a glimmer of consolation, allowing her to justify to herself the lack of responses.

Meanwhile, Jordan is in a complicated situation. After experiencing moments of vulnerability with Ethan, he decides it is time to end that unexpected visit. Firmly, but without wanting to delve into the discussion of what happened, he asks Ethan to leave the apartment. He doesn't want to waste time rehashing the past or explaining his reasons; he only feels the urgency to put his life and thoughts in order.

Once alone, Jordan faces the dilemma of how to communicate with Avery. The realization of having spent the night in such an unexpected way makes it difficult for him to explain without fully disclosing the situation. After pondering for a moment, he decides to send a message to Avery, opting for an excuse that can explain his silence without arousing suspicion. Carefully, he chooses his words, hoping to maintain the nascent trust between them, yet feeling the weight of the unspoken truth.

"Good morning dear Avery and happy lunchtime, given the hour... I'm sorry for only responding now, but I just woke up after a sleepless night. I hope you're doing well. How was the dinner with your friend last night? Today I really need to focus on work to make up for lost time, but I would very much like to talk tonight. A kiss, see you soon."

As soon as Avery receives the notification of Jordan's message, she opens it with a mix of anxiety and impatience. Reading his words, a sense of relief envelops her.

"Just as I imagined, he stayed up all night... poor thing," she thinks with an affectionate smile.

"Perfect, then I'll call him tonight." This small confirmation makes her feel closer to Jordan, reassured by knowing that the reasons for his silence were simply due to the need to recuperate after a difficult night. With a lighter heart, Avery prepares to resume her daily activities, already excitedly thinking about the evening conversation with Jordan.

Meanwhile, an idea strikes Avery: she wants to start creating a playlist to share with Jordan. Not yet knowing his musical tastes in detail, she decides this will be one of the topics of their next conversation. Intrigued by the opportunity to discover another aspect of Jordan's personality through music, Avery feels excited about the idea of putting together a selection of songs that can accompany their moments of sharing, both virtual and, perhaps one day, real. This project becomes another way for her to forge closer ties with Jordan, exploring together the melodies that resonate with their emotions and experiences.

Feeling an urgent need to get some fresh air, Jordan decides to go outside. The idea of staying within four walls suffocates him; he feels that only the open air can offer him some relief. As he walks, his thoughts are in turmoil. He is torn by uncertainty: should he be honest with Avery about the events of the past night, or would it be better to let it go, pretending nothing happened?

The decision weighs on him like a boulder. On one hand, honesty could strengthen their bond, showing Avery that he trusts her enough to share difficult moments. On the other, he fears that revealing he spent time with Ethan could somehow crack the trust or create unwanted misunderstandings.

As he moves beyond the familiar streets, Jordan reflects on how important Avery has become to him in such a short time. He realizes he doesn't want to lose the special connection they have built. Perhaps, he thinks, the best way forward is to find a balance between honesty and caution, perhaps mentioning his sleeplessness without going into too much detail, at least for now.

Meanwhile, he decides to send a message to Avery, not so much to talk about what happened, but to feel close to her, even just virtually.
"I'm going out for a walk, need to clear my head a bit. Talking to you always helps me sort out my thoughts. Hope to hear from you soon," he writes, hoping this gesture can somehow make up for the silence and uncertainty that have characterized the last few hours.

Knock Knock... may I? There's a knock at the door and, with a mix of surprise and joy, Avery exclaims:
"Axel! What a surprise, how nice to see you! Come in!" She welcomes him with a warm hug and a kiss on the cheek, expressing all her happiness at seeing him again.
"Look at you, never aging, eh?" she teases affectionately.
"You're always flattering and not entirely honest, Avery," responds Axel with a smile, holding her tight for a moment.
"I thought, since you struggle to pull away from work... here I am. Hope I'm not intruding."

"Not at all, it's a wonderful surprise! How long has it been since we last had a drink together? Six months?" Avery inquires.
"I must correct you, it's been almost a year," Axel points out, inducing a sense of guilt in Avery for the time that has flown by so quickly.
"A year? Really?" she exclaims, surprised.
"Then, to make it up to you, how about lunch at Il Gattopardo?" she generously proposes.

"No Il Gattopardo today, Avery. That's more a place for business meetings. Today should be something more special, don't you think? Let's go to a beach club on the bay instead. When was the last time you set foot on a beach?" Axel suggests with enthusiasm.

"What a fantastic idea, Axel... I'm not dressed for the beach, but that's alright. Just give me twenty minutes and I'll be ready," Avery responds, ready to leave her work worries behind for a few hours.

As Avery finishes up some tasks on the computer and handles a couple of phone calls, Axel can't help but notice how enchanting she still is. He enjoyed watching her talk, the way she moved her hands, how she fixed that rebellious tuft of hair, or the concentrated expression that furrowed her brows.
"Damn, Avery, how do you still make my heart beat this fast..." thinks Axel, as he grabs his jacket and they prepare to leave.

Despite the feelings he had for her since their university days, he had always chosen to remain silent so as not to jeopardize their special bond, keeping his love a secret.

The virtual hug

"Mmmh, these shrimp are delicious, and the rice salad? I had forgotten how good it is to eat in these small restaurants by the bay," exclaims Avery, clearly delighted by the meal.
"Well, I guess you're used to gourmet restaurants by now," jokes Axel, exaggerating refined manners.
"Oh, don't caricature me, I'm not a snob at all," Avery retorts lightly.

Then, changing the subject, Axel asks with a mix of curiosity and a hint of veiled jealousy:
"What about this story with the artist from the virtual gallery, what can you tell me?"
"The artist, as you call him, is named Jordan," corrects Avery, "he's really a special person: intelligent, sensitive, and surprisingly mature. A few days ago, we exchanged phone numbers, so now we can communicate privately, as is the fashion today. This new friendship really makes me feel good; it was just what I needed."

"No, Avery, what you really need is right here, in front of you," Axel would have liked to tell her, expressing the feelings he had long harbored in his heart. However, as often happens, he finds himself playing the role of friend and confidant, listening to Avery's romantic stories without ever revealing the true affection he feels for her, keeping his own desires hidden and continuing to support her as he always has.

Back in the privacy of his apartment, Jordan lets out a gesture of frustration, ripping the sheets off the bed, still imbued with the scent of the previous night. With mechanical movements, he starts the laundry and then stands in front of one of his most recent artworks. As he gazes at the canvas, a thought crosses his mind:
"What if I left everything behind? This city isn't even my home. Ethan wouldn't know where to find me, and I could finally put an end to this toxic relationship."

The idea of seeking help from Avery fleetingly crosses his mind.
"Maybe she could offer me some advice, help me find a new place to start over." But he almost immediately dismisses the idea, recognizing the need to face this phase of his life alone.
"No, I shouldn't depend on someone else again. I need to find my own way without involving her," he convinces himself. Determined to keep his dilemma a secret, he decides not to reveal anything to Avery, preferring to face the challenge of a new beginning alone.

"Hi Jordan, I hope I'm not disturbing you. Is it a tough time? The whole day has gone by without us talking, and I really missed your voice..." Avery begins, with a hint of concern in her voice.
"Avery, it's so good to hear from you, I really needed your call," responds Jordan, revealing a mix of tiredness and relief.
"Today has been a busy day, full of reflections, new projects, and constant thoughts of you."

"Jordan, you sound tired. Can I do something for you? Did something specific happen?" Avery insists, sensing the weariness in his voice.
"Nothing worrisome. And you? How was your day?" Jordan tries to divert, seeking to lighten the conversation's tone.

"Just a normal day, with work and commitments. I'm organizing a vernissage for the business center and would like to display some of your works. The event is in 6 months, but these things take time to organize well. Could you send me a PDF catalog? So we could choose the artworks to exhibit together," Avery suggests, trying to involve Jordan in a shared project.

"Of course, Avery, I'll send it as soon as possible. Thanks a lot for this opportunity," responds Jordan, grateful. Then, with a hint of daring, he adds:
"By the way, how about a video call one of these days? It would be nice to finally see each other..." Avery is surprised by the proposal, not expecting such a direct approach.
"A video call? Honestly, I hadn't felt the need. I'll think about it," she responds hesitantly.

"Sorry, I didn't mean to make you uncomfortable," Jordan quickly apologizes.
"We can keep communicating as we have been, and when you feel ready, you can let me know," he suggests, showing understanding and patience.
"Thanks for understanding," says Avery, reassured by his sensitivity.

Jordan, aware of the distance separating him from Avery and the limitations imposed by their digital communication, gently expresses his longing for a more intimate connection.

"Although it's not possible to see you in person," he confides with a gentle tone, "I wish you could feel my presence next to you, imagine your hands in mine," whispers Jordan, daring a little more.

"If you close your eyes, you can feel me right beside you," he adds. Avery closes her eyes, surrendering to the imagination of Jordan as a tall, strong, and protective man, a bulwark against the adversities of the world.

But just in this moment of sweet exaltation, Avery begins to slide into the trap of idealization. It's normal, at the beginning of getting to know someone, to idealize the other person, seeing only their positive aspects and ignoring the flaws. This tendency to create a perfect and unattainable image of the other is often linked to low self-esteem, turning the potential partner into an unreachable ideal rather than a real person with strengths and weaknesses.

"It's really a nice feeling...almost like a hug for the soul...I want to fall asleep with this sweet image of us, Jordan... Goodnight. A kiss, see you tomorrow," responds Avery, enveloped in an emotional warmth she had not felt in a long time.
"Goodnight, dear Avery, sweet dreams," replies Jordan, finally finding comfort and peace in that strange day.

The proposal

"What an incredible dream," thinks Avery the following morning, "it felt so real." She was in her first apartment where she had moved to live alone, but the colors were very vivid, completely different from what she remembered.
In the living room, there was a person: a perfect stranger, but his presence didn't disturb her.

As she walks towards the strange guest, she realizes she is not alone; Jordan appears at her side. He is enveloped in a soft light, which gently accentuates his features, making him simultaneously familiar and mysterious. Jordan smiles at her, offering his hand, and together they continue to walk out of the house toward the garden.
The stranger gets up and follows them, no one speaks.
The scene then opens in a cozy café, where she and Jordan are sharing a moment of intimacy, surrounded by light laughter and affectionate glances. The atmosphere is warm, familiar, and a fluid, passionate conversation flows between them, seeming to bring them even closer.

Suddenly, the dream takes an unexpected turn: Jordan, with a serious yet gentle expression, tells her that he has something important to say and asks her to meet him in his office before disappearing.

Avery gets ready carefully for the appointment. She wears her favorite dress and, before leaving, takes a look in the mirror, making sure she is ready to see Jordan. With determined steps, she heads towards her car, but as soon as she tries to start it, the vehicle remains motionless, as if lifeless. She repeatedly tries to turn the key in the ignition, but without success.

Trying to stay calm, she takes out her cellphone from her purse to call Jordan and inform him of the setback, but discovers that the phone also seems to be out of service. No signal, no possibility to make calls or send messages. The frustration grows, and with it, a sense of helplessness.

It is in this moment of confusion that a male figure reappears; the stranger approaches with a sure step.
"Do you need help?" he asks, with a voice surprisingly familiar. Avery turns to look at him and, although the man's face is blurred, the voice is unmistakable: it's Axel's.

At the moment when the stranger-Axel offers to help, the dream dissolves. This strange meeting in the dream, the car that won't start, the silent phone, and finally the appearance of Axel at a moment of need, all contribute to a sense of disorientation that persists even after waking up.

"Good morning, Jordan. How was your night? You know, you appeared in a dream I had? It was so vivid it seemed real... You had to tell me something very important, but then, for some reason, we couldn't meet again..." Avery enhances her message with a series of smiling emoticons and kisses, trying to lighten the tone and share the memory of her dream casually.

Jordan, on his part, had not had a good night. There's a saying that when we can't sleep, it's because we're awake in someone else's dreams... And indeed, he was awake, reflecting on the emotional turmoil of the night just passed, when his phone emits the sound of a notification, revealing Avery's message.

The coincidence between his state of insomnia and Avery's dream brings a bitter smile to his face.

"Maybe there's some truth to that legend," he thinks, as he types a response, trying to hide the tiredness and emotional disarray that had accompanied him during the dark hours. However, Avery's sweetness offers him a moment of distraction and peace, a small refuge from the tumult of his thoughts.

"Good morning, Avery! I hope you started your day on the right foot! My night? Well, let's just say it was eventful, but reading about your dream brought me a smile. It's curious how the mind travels while the body rests, don't you think? Yes, it seems dreams have their own way of bringing us together, even when reality keeps us apart. Who knows, maybe next time we'll be able to finish that interrupted conversation! A kiss and may your day be as wonderful as you are!"

With this message, Jordan tries to maintain a positive and lively tone, hoping to convey some morning cheer to Avery. However, behind the facade of enthusiasm, he skillfully hides his melancholy, a sentiment that dominated his restless night.

Jordan has always had a melancholic soul and a deeply private nature. In times of discomfort, he tends to retreat into himself, pushing away even those closest to him. This way of being was one of the main reasons for the end of his relationship with Ethan. Often, Jordan gets lost in the meanders of his thoughts, building mental prisons from which he struggles to escape. Only painting has the power to unlock him and bring him serenity, but even this refuge is experienced in complete solitude.

He doesn't want Avery to see this darker side of him. He aims to always present himself in the best light to her, displaying an enthusiasm and vitality that he often doesn't truly feel. For Jordan, maintaining this facade is not particularly challenging; it only takes pressing a few keys and fabricating. This ability to hide his true state of mind behind messages full of life and optimism has become second nature to him, a defense mechanism to protect himself and the people he cares about from coming into contact with his more vulnerable side.

Jordan thinks about how to keep Avery's attention on him while also diverting his mind from his melancholic moods and finally has an idea that seems perfect.
Eager to offer something new and exciting, he considers proposing to Avery to explore virtual environments together, where users can create and live through avatars, exploring identity and relationships in new and creative ways.

In these worlds, it is possible to experience romantic or sexual encounters in a safe and controlled setting, allowing users to freely experiment with different aspects of their personality and relationships in a protected and imaginative environment. Jordan sees this opportunity as a way to explore new dimensions of their relationship, without the pressures or complexities of the real world.

Determined to propose this adventure to Avery, Jordan already imagines the endless possibilities that these virtual spaces could offer them as a couple, allowing them to share unique experiences and perhaps even reveal hidden sides of their personalities in a playful and non-judgmental context.

Before sending the message with his proposal, Jordan ponders how to present the idea in a way that is inviting and exciting, without scaring or embarrassing Avery. He wants it to be a shared experience, an adventure that could enrich their connection and offer new insights into their mutual understanding.

With a mix of excitement and a hint of nervousness, Jordan types the message, hoping that Avery will enthusiastically accept his proposal and that together they can embark on these new virtual explorations, discovering together what it truly means to connect in a boundless world.

"Hello Avery,

I hope this day is smiling upon you. While reflecting on new ways to explore and deepen our connection, an idea occurred to me that I hope you will find intriguing.

Have you ever heard of virtual environments like NeoHorizon? They are virtual worlds where people can create avatars to explore identities, relationships, and experiences in creative and new ways. I was wondering... how would you feel about venturing together into this virtual space? It could be a fun and safe way to experience different aspects of our personalities and our relationships, all in a controlled and liberating environment.

Through avatars, we could share romantic experiences, or even just exploratory ones, in scenarios that would be impossible or impractical in real life. I think it could be a unique opportunity to get to know each other better, in a context different from the usual, and perhaps discover new sides of each other.

Of course, the proposal might seem a bit unconventional, but I believe it could be an exciting experience for both of us. And who knows, maybe we'll find surprising ways to interact and express our feelings in this parallel world.

Let me know what you think. If the idea intrigues you, I'm here to explore this new universe with you. And, of course, if you prefer to keep our interactions as they are now, that's perfectly fine with me too. The most important thing for me is that we feel comfortable and happy in our relationship, whatever form it may take.

I eagerly await your response.

Warm regards,
Jordan"

A Dive into the Unknown: Avery's Virtual Discovery

"The idea of the video call wasn't so bad after all," thinks Avery after reading Jordan's message. Now she finds herself in a whirlwind of conflicting emotions. The idea of exploring the metaverse and immersing herself in a fully virtual world deeply intrigues her, but at the same time, it intimidates her. She has never dealt with environments like NeoHorizon and is not sure how to navigate these alternative realities, nor the rules that govern them, if there are any.

The prospect of having to create an avatar and then interact in such a complex world causes her palpable anxiety. Avery is aware of how even the simplest technological operations can sometimes become sources of stress, making her feel inadequate and incapable. The idea of managing a virtual identity and relating through it on the web seems to her a daunting and complex task, well beyond her capabilities.

However, reflecting on these fears, Avery realizes that her reaction is a classic example of self-sabotage. She is used to belittling herself and convincing herself she is not capable, even before trying. This realization hits her hard; she notices how often she has allowed unfounded insecurities to hold her back, preventing herself from exploring new experiences and growing.

With a mix of trepidation and determination, Avery decides not to be overcome by her fears. She recognizes that Jordan's invitation is an opportunity to challenge her insecurities, to learn something new, and most importantly, to deepen their connection in an original and creative way. She decides to respond to Jordan, expressing her curiosity and her concerns, open to exploring this new universe with him while admitting her doubts and anxiety about facing the unknown.

"Hello Jordan,

I read your message this morning and I must say that your proposal caught me a bit off guard, but in a positive way. The idea of exploring virtual environments like NeoHorizon together is completely new to me and, I must admit, it intrigues me a lot. The possibility of experiencing and exploring new aspects of our personalities in such a creative context sounds really fascinating.

However, I cannot deny feeling some apprehension. I am not very experienced with these kinds of technologies, and the idea of creating an avatar and interacting in a virtual world makes me a bit anxious. Sometimes, even downloading an app can seem like a big deal to me, so you can imagine how I feel like a novice in front of all this.

But then I thought about it and realized that, in the end, my hesitation is just a way of convincing myself that I'm not capable before even trying. And I don't want fear to prevent me from having new experiences or from deepening our understanding and connection.

So, here I am, telling you that... I accept your proposal. I am ready to dive into this adventure with you, despite my doubts. It will be an opportunity to learn, grow, and, I hope, have fun together. I believe that, with your guidance, I can overcome my uncertainties, and maybe we will discover sides of ourselves that we still do not know.

So yes, let's do it. But please, be patient with me. I will be like a child taking their first steps in an unknown world, so I will need your support and understanding along the way.

Thank you for proposing this adventure. I look forward to starting and seeing where it will take us.

Warm regards,
Avery"

Currently, Avery faces an exciting challenge: a new project to carry forward. Jordan's innovative proposal has the potential to completely revolutionize her daily routine, a prospect that stimulates her as much as it intimidates her. To feel adequately prepared and confident, Avery decides to delve into the exploration of the metaverse, a concept still nebulous to her. Sitting comfortably in front of her computer, she begins thorough research, eager to discover everything there is to know about this virtual reality that is gaining increasing popularity.

Here is the information that Avery finds during her research:

Definition of Metaverse: The metaverse is described as a collective set of connected virtual spaces, where people can interact through avatars in three-dimensional environments. It extends beyond individual games or platforms, creating a parallel digital universe that integrates aspects of social, professional, and entertainment life.

Avery learns that there are various metaverse platforms, each with its own peculiarities. NeoHorizon, Roblox, and Decentraland are mentioned as notable examples, each offering different experiences, from exploring fantastical worlds to participating in virtual events and building personal spaces.

It is explained how users can create and customize their avatars to represent themselves in the metaverse. This process includes selecting physical features, clothing, and accessories, allowing each user to express their individuality.

Avery also learns that the metaverse offers endless possibilities for social interaction, such as chatting, attending virtual meetings, exploring immersive environments together, and much more. The research reveals that immersion in the metaverse is made possible by advanced technologies, including VR (Virtual Reality) headsets, sensor gloves, and haptic suits. These tools enable a richer and more engaging experience, making users feel as if they are physically present in the virtual world.

Avery also finds important discussions on privacy, security, and ethical issues in the metaverse. The need to protect one's personal information and to navigate safely in these spaces becomes evident.

With this information, she feels more prepared to navigate the complex and fascinating universe of the metaverse. The knowledge gained gives her the confidence needed to further explore the potential of this new project proposed by Jordan, with a critical eye but also with great curiosity for the innovations it could bring to her life.

"Hello Jordan! I've done some research on the metaverse, and I must say I'm quite excited about the idea of exploring it. It seems like the next big step in our way of interacting online... First, though, I need your advice: which software should I download to start? I want to make sure I make the right choice for our virtual adventure."

"Hello Avery! I'm glad to hear you're ready to explore the metaverse with me, I wasn't sure about proposing all this at the beginning... As for the software, it depends a bit on what we're looking to do... Personally, I would suggest starting with VRChat. It offers a wide variety of worlds and experiences, and it's great for full immersion."

"Wow, you really know a lot about this subject! And to think I had pictured you as a somewhat nostalgic painter, lost in sunsets. Anyway, VRChat seems like a great choice to start with. Thank you so much for suggesting it! Now, I'm considering buying some accessories to fully immerse myself in the experience: VR headsets, sensor gloves, and maybe even a haptic suit. What do you think? Any advice? Am I going too fast?"

"Ah, Avery, I like to surprise! Yes, painting and sunsets have their charm, but exploring new virtual worlds has its own unique appeal. As for the gear, I think you're doing a great job preparing for a full immersion. The DreamLens headset is essential, and the VisionSphere Pro is a versatile option that offers good value for money. Sensor gloves and a haptic suit definitely enhance the immersion, but they also represent a bigger investment. I'd say start with the headset and then, based on how you feel, decide whether and how much to expand the equipment. You're not moving too fast at all; you're just enthusiastic, and that's wonderful!"

"So, Avery, for the headset, I highly recommend the VisionSphere Pro. It strikes a good balance between quality and price, and it also works standalone, so you don't need a high-end computer to use it. However, if you want a richer experience, you can connect it to a PC. Regarding sensor gloves and the haptic suit, you should know that the choices are less varied and tend to be quite expensive. The HapticSuit Nexus and TouchWave Armor are excellent for tactile feedback and immersion. I suggest starting with the headset and seeing how you feel before thinking about expanding your set."

"Got it, I'll look into DreamLens and then consider the other accessories. Thanks a lot for the tips, Jordan! I'm really excited about embarking on this virtual adventure together. I'll keep you updated on my purchases and, once I'm equipped, let's organize to meet online!"

"Fantastic, Avery! If you need more info or help setting everything up, I'm here for you. Exploring the metaverse together will be incredible. See you soon in our new world! Take care."

Avery's Dilemma

Avery found herself immersed in online research so intensely that she spent almost the entire morning without even realizing it, completely neglecting her scheduled commitments. To further complicate matters, she had put her phone on silent mode, making her unaware of Tessa's repeated calls.

"Oh no, I can't believe it, I've been glued to the screen for almost three hours!" she exclaims, realizing with dismay how much time she had actually wasted.

In the confusion of the moment, Avery quickly gets ready, putting on the first clothes she finds and grabbing only her work bag, forgetting the other bag placed on the pouf near the entrance. The afternoon turns into a marathon of phone calls: Avery spends hours apologizing to her contacts, trying to justify her absence with improbable excuses and attempting to reschedule the missed appointments. Tessa, witnessing this unusual series of events, looks at Avery with a mix of surprise and incredulity.

She had never seen her act with such ease in weaving through lies and excuses, a behavior completely out of the ordinary for her.

Meanwhile, Jordan is navigating his basement; moving to a smaller apartment had forced him to give up the comfort of a spacious gamer setup that he once proudly arranged in his parents' house.

There, he had dedicated an entire room to gaming, equipping it with an ergonomic chair, a lumbar cushion, a footrest, high-quality headphones, and, of course, an impressive screen. Now, these pieces of equipment became precious again for the adventure he was about to embark on with Avery. "It must be somewhere... the headset, my last purchase... I'm sure I grouped everything together," Jordan mutters, rummaging through boxes in a damp and dusty corner.

"Tessa, I'm really sorry about this morning," Avery begins in a timid voice, "it's just that Lorraine stopped by, and we had to sort out some issues related to the divorce. You know how anxious all this makes me, and I simply lost track of time."

Avery finds herself making up this excuse on the spot, preferring not to admit that she got distracted searching for VR headsets online... That detail had to remain a secret between her and Jordan.

"Don't worry, Avery," responds Tessa with a sigh of resignation, "but next time let me know if you need time for your personal matters, so I can arrange to help you. I'm here for that."

"I know, you're my go-to person," assures Avery, "I promise to keep you informed in the future."

As she speaks, Avery begins to look for her bag.

"Ah, Tessa, have you seen my bag? I can't find it anywhere. It has the office keys, house keys, remotes... but where did I leave it?" she complains, searching in all the rooms of the office.

"I don't think you had it with you when you arrived today," replies Tessa, "are you sure you didn't leave it in the car?"

"No, I took a taxi because I was late... oh no, now I remember, I left it at home... and now what do I do?" Avery despairs.
"But Avery, haven't you left a set of keys with someone for emergencies like this?" Tessa presses.

"Tessa, you're a genius! Of course, Axel has a spare set. I'll call him right away. Could you please close up the office? See you tomorrow!"

"Alright, see you tomorrow, Avery." With a sense of urgency, Avery calls Axel: "Hi, sorry to bother you at this hour, but I have a favor to ask..."

"Hi Avery, no problem, I'm still working. What's up?" Axel responds with curiosity.
"Well, I left my bag at home this morning with everything in it, including my house key... I'm locked out," Avery confesses.

"Ahaha, really?" Axel bursts out laughing, finding the situation quite amusing.

"Please, Axel, stop joking, I'm already embarrassed enough having to call you for something like this!" Avery exclaims, trying to keep the tone light.
"Let's face it, you're just looking for an excuse to spend more time with me; imagine, seeing each other twice in one week!" he replies, continuing to tease her.
"Okay, okay, keep laughing. But after you've finished, could you do me a big favor and bring me my house keys?" asks Avery, trying to hide her embarrassment.

"Ok... but first tell me, have you eaten yet?" Axel surprises her with his question.
"What?" Avery is visibly confused.
"Eating, Avery, you know, that fundamental activity for our survival," he insists in a joking tone.
"No, obviously not. The day has been a disaster, and I've been in the office until now," she confesses, revealing how caught up she was with work.
"Perfect, I haven't had dinner either. How about we grab something to eat together before I take you home?" proposes Axel kindly.
"You're an angel, Axel," Avery can't help but smile.
"I know, see you soon," he concludes, ready to turn the evening into something positive.

During dinner, Avery opens up to Axel, sharing the latest updates about the situation with Lorraine and some news about Jordan, carefully omitting details about the headset and her explorations of virtual reality.

Axel, however, seems distant, lost in his thoughts. He has known Avery for three decades, having been by her side through ups and downs, moments of joy, and difficult periods. Now that Avery is free, he realizes he can no longer deny his feelings. He loves her deeply, captivated by her brilliant mind, her determination, her eyes always full of wonder, and her mouth that silently invites kisses.

"Hey Axel, shall we get dessert?" Avery's voice abruptly brings him back to the present.
"Did you listen to what I said? Where were you with your thoughts?" He apologizes, explaining that he was distracted, while Avery lists the dessert options: apple pie, brownies with vanilla ice cream, red velvet cake, and Boston cream pie.
"You know I'm not a big fan of sweets, you choose; maybe I'll have a bit of yours," replies Axel, trying to mask his inner turmoil.

"Okay, maybe I'll take the brownies with ice cream. But are you okay? You've been very quiet tonight."

"Sorry Avery. I was just thinking about how we share the same city yet rarely see each other. Your 'distraction' this morning was a great excuse to meet up. We really should do it more often."

"Come on, don't be like that. It's true, we've lost touch a bit, but don't you find it incredible how, despite everything, our friendship remains intact? It's like no time passes when we're together."

"You're right, Avery. There has always been a kind of magic between us. Even if months pass without seeing each other, when we do meet, it's as if we were together the day before. Our connection is really special."

"Yes, it is. Thanks again for this evening, Axel. And for coming to my rescue, as always."
"It's always a pleasure, Avery. You know you can count on me. And... let's not let life take away moments like these."

The conversation between Avery and Axel reveals not just the depth of their friendship but also Axel's unexpressed feelings. Despite the distractions and moments of silence, the bond they share is palpable, evidencing a connection that withstands time and circumstances.

Avery stops in front of her house. "Axel, why don't you come up for one last drink? I can also give you the keys back. I'd feel better knowing they're with you again."

"Sure, why not? One last drink sounds good."

They enter the house, and Avery says, "Could you open a bottle of red? I'll just take a moment to water the plants. This place is becoming a jungle, but I love having all these plants around."

"Okay, I'll find the wine. Take all the time you need."

After a few minutes, they are both on the couch with a nice glass of wine, Avery has made herself comfortable in grey pajamas and funny yellow socks, while Axel begins to speak with determination.

"Avery, there's something I need to tell you. I've been trying to find the courage... I have feelings for you. Not just as friends. I admire you, I'm more attracted to you than I've ever admitted. And I wonder if... if you might feel something similar."

"Axel, I don't know what to say. I'm... surprised. I had never considered... I mean, maybe there were some signs, but I never thought it could be real. I never wanted to admit it, not even to myself."

"I understand this puts you in a difficult position. I don't want to pressure you. I just needed you to know how I feel. You're important to me, Avery, no matter what."

"It's not... it's not about pressure. It's just that I wasn't expecting it. I need a moment to... process all of this. Axel, you're one of the most important people in my life. I don't want to lose you."

"And you won't lose me. We're friends first and foremost, right? Whatever you decide, it won't change the fact that I care about you, Avery. I just wanted to be honest about my feelings."

Axel's revelation opens a door to new possibilities between them, leaving Avery to ponder feelings she may have ignored or suppressed.

Meanwhile, Jordan reflects on a melody echoing in his mind, a song from a few years back but still enchanting.
"This piece should touch her; it's a wonderful song, I wonder what effect it could have on Avery," he thinks. He decides to write to her, aware of the late hour and assuming Avery is already deep in sleep.

"Dear Avery,

I wanted to hear your voice before closing my eyes for the night, but work captivated me more than expected, and only now do I realize how late it is. I'm sending you this song, hoping it can give you a sweet awakening. A big hug. Yours, Jordan."

Avery's phone chimes with the notification of the message just as Axel gathers the necessary courage, moving closer to Avery to gently take the wine glass from her hands and kiss her. Struck by a mix of emotions, perhaps due to the stress accumulated during the day or the effect of the wine, Avery does not push Axel away but instead embraces him more tightly.

During those moments, Avery finds herself torn between two diametrically opposed emotions. On one hand, her upbringing had imprinted on her a certain social role, where a woman should never yield to her desires for mere pleasure or personal enjoyment. For Avery, the topic of sexuality had always been taboo; her conservative environment and Catholic education had shaped her to be the devoted spouse, always ready to fulfill her husband's demands without hesitation, making him feel satisfied, even if it often meant finding solace in the loneliness of autoeroticism to satisfy her own needs and desires.

On the other hand, she discovers a body that can finally free itself from shame, claiming the right to pure physical enjoyment. She gives in to Axel's kisses and skillful caresses, which expertly explore her body, from her breasts to her hips, down to her belly, awakening in her sensations that had been dormant until then.

"We did something very wrong," Avery confesses to Axel after unexpected intimacy when the intensity of the moment and the effects of dopamine and oxytocin begin to fade. "What were we thinking, Axel? We're friends, we shouldn't have crossed that line."

"But Avery, I told you clearly how I felt about you. You knew that my feelings went beyond just friendship," Axel retorts seriously, starting to get dressed.

"And to be honest, you didn't seem to mind a few hours ago."

"That's a low blow, Axel. Is that all you have to say, besides these platitudes?" Avery rebukes him, trying to defend herself.
"I'm not ready for such an intense relationship."

"Of course," responds Axel with a hint of bitterness.
"It's better to continue chatting with someone you don't even know in person."

"Please, Axel, leave me alone now. I'm sorry, I didn't say it's all your fault. We are both responsible, but I don't have the strength to talk about this right now," Avery defends herself, tired.

"Avery," says Axel, sitting next to her and gently taking her hands.
"I will leave now, giving you time to think. I want you to know that you are and remain a special person to me, and nothing has changed on my part. Goodnight." He leaves a kiss on her forehead before leaving, leaving Avery to reflect on the complexity of their shared feelings and the uncertainties of the future.

"I can't believe it," Avery exclaims with a sigh, feeling overwhelmed by recent events.

"It almost feels like the universe is having fun testing me," she reflects while reading the message from Jordan and listening to the song he sent, "If You Don't Know Me by Now" by Simply Red. Avery's surprise is tangible because the song Jordan dedicated to her is the same one she shared during her engagement years with Eric, a coincidence that catches her completely off guard.

Hearing those notes, filled with memories and past emotions, in such a different context, makes her feel a mix of nostalgia and wonder. Jordan's unwitting choice of that particular song as a dedication for her opens a gateway for reflection on the unexpected continuity of emotional experiences in her life, revealing how the past can intertwine with the present in surprising and unpredictable ways.

"Incredible..." Avery's mind is still troubled by all the events of that strange day.

"Here it comes again," she murmurs, referring to the guilt that seems to peek back in.

"And now what do I do? Should I talk to Jordan about it? After all, we are not officially a couple... I don't want a relationship to start this way. Maybe it's not right to tell him via message; better to call him when I'm in the office. Perhaps he can help me see my feelings more clearly," she reflects, looking at the two still full glasses on the living room table, silent witnesses of a complicated evening.

Melodies, Metaverse and New Beginnings

"Hi Jordan, we can finally have a moment to ourselves. Do you have time to talk now?" Avery begins with a note of relief in her voice.

"Hi Avery, you know there's always time for you," responds Jordan warmly.

"Thank you for the song, it's really special and touching. How did you come across it? It's not exactly from your generation," jokes Avery, trying to lighten the tone of the conversation.

"I'm glad you liked it. After all, beauty doesn't belong to an era... and besides, listening to Mozart doesn't mean you have to live in the eighteenth century!" replies Jordan, playing with words.

"You're absolutely right. I must say I admire your taste in music... You know, I thought of making a playlist for you too. Maybe I've ruined the surprise now, but at least I know I can include some older songs," shares Avery, a bit embarrassed but happy to share the thought.

"Really? That sounds like there's a special connection between us..." comments Jordan, highlighting the depth of their bond.

"And how did it go yesterday? Were you able to install the software we talked about?" asks Jordan, curious about Avery's progress in the virtual world.

"Yes, I've almost finished everything. I just need to create my account and then I'll be ready to explore with my avatar." As if I don't already have enough complications in real life... Avery thinks and smiles bitterly at the thought.

"I also made some purchases; I'll let you know as soon as everything arrives. Yesterday, I was so engrossed in this project that I skipped work... imagine the chaos."

"Really? You must have been really caught up. What happened then?" Jordan inquires, intrigued.

"Well, I had to reschedule some appointments, making up the most improbable excuses. I forgot my bag at home, so I was locked out... luckily, Axel had a spare key," concludes Avery, emphasizing the absurdity and intensity of her day.
"..about Axel..." Avery starts, feeling the need to share the incident with Jordan, "you know, he was the one who suggested I explore that virtual gallery where I discovered your works."

"Oh really?" responds Jordan, interested. "Then I should contact him and offer something to thank him for it."

Thanking doesn't seem quite the right word!... Avery thinks, surprised by how fate can play such cruel jokes... and she feels it's not the right time to go further, lacking the courage to tell everything.

"I've known Axel for a lifetime, he's one of those people I can always count on, that's why he has a spare set of my house keys."

"Well, it's a good thing he was there, then," continues Jordan, understanding.
"Unfortunately, I can't be there physically to help you like he can, but whenever you want to talk, remember that I'm here for you, at any hour."

"Jordan..." Avery seems to be searching for the right words.

"Tell me, Avery," he urges.

"I can't wait to meet you, even if only virtually."

"It will happen soon, Avery, and it will be fun. Shall we talk tonight?"

"Sure, call me whenever you want."

"Then, tonight it is, a kiss Avery."

"Bye Jordan, a kiss." Avery ends the call, internally reproaching herself for not having the courage to tell everything to Jordan.

"Tomorrow I'll come to pick up my things," Avery reads on her phone screen. Finally, Eric has decided to take that step. This will give her the chance to reorganize the studio, she thinks, allowing her to work from another computer and keep everything she needs at hand without having to occupy the living room. Although she doesn't have a stream of people in her house, she prefers to prevent any unwanted questions.

"Great, Jordan's PDF is ready. Now I can select some of his works to organize the shipment," reflects Avery, eager for every detail of the vernissage to be impeccable. After all, she knows that sooner or later she will meet Jordan face-to-face, even if for now she prefers to set aside the thought.

She notices she has three unread messages from Axel. It's not like her to ignore people, especially him.

"I'll reply to him later, calmly," she promises herself, continuing to browse through the images in Jordan's catalog, focused on her work but with her mind occasionally drifting to the complex web of her personal relationships.

"These works are perfect, I'll suggest them to Jordan. If he agrees, we'll include them in the vernissage," Avery reflects, immersed in her work. This commitment allows her to bring her mind back to the present and keep other thoughts at bay.

When she arrives home, she finds several packages waiting for her in the mailbox. "Wow, that was fast!" she exclaims, surprised, as she opens the parcels. The DreamLens headset and the webcam have already arrived. Now it's time to focus on creating her avatar.

Sitting in front of the computer, Avery begins the process: she enters an email address, chooses a username, and sets a password. During the registration, she is asked to select a base avatar, which she can later customize.

"Let's see," says Avery, as the browser requests access to the camera. She clicks "Allow" in the top left corner and takes a photo with good lighting, capturing her facial features clearly.
"Okay, let's move on," she continues.

The next step is choosing the gender of the avatar. Avery notices that she can only modify two aspects initially: the skin color, by clicking on the droplet-shaped icon, and the color of the clothes, by selecting the shirt icon. "For now, this is fine," Avery decides, planning to make more detailed customizations later.

Jordan is skilled at navigating the web and has already built his personal corner in the metaverse, equipped with an avatar that looks nothing like his real appearance. He likes the idea of transforming completely into someone else; after all, these virtual spaces offer the freedom to experiment.
"Maybe Avery will also find it fun to create an entirely different avatar," Jordan reflects, curious to see what she will do.

"Hi Avery, am I disturbing you, or was there something you were doing?" Jordan asks over the phone, always careful not to sound intrusive.

"Hi Jordan, no, you've come at just the right time. I've just signed up and created my first avatar, which I think I'll modify later. It's been quite fun," replies Avery, enthusiastically.

"And I have some news to share with you: tomorrow, Eric, my ex, will come to pick up his things. I've decided to transform the room full of boxes into my new office for online activities," adds Avery, with a hint of satisfaction in her voice.

"Great decision, Avery. See, little by little, everything is getting sorted out. It's a good way to finally close that chapter of your life," comments Jordan, offering her support and encouragement.

"By the way, Avery, the works you've selected are exactly the ones I was thinking of too. It's perfect for me, then you'll have to explain to me in detail how to organize a vernissage," says Jordan, curious to learn more.

"So, you agree? Fantastic, Jordan, you won't be disappointed. We'll need to prepare a new catalog for the event, create posters, brochures, and business cards... but don't worry, I'll take care of everything. You'll see, you're going to be famous and receive the recognition you deserve," responds Avery, full of enthusiasm.

"Regarding the invitations, if you're okay with it, we could also inform your parents. What do you think?" she adds, suggesting involving Jordan's family in the event.

"I'm not sure," Jordan replies, his voice suddenly more serious. "It's been a long time since we last saw or even spoke to each other. We haven't even exchanged birthday or holiday greetings in the last few years."

"Well, you have a 50% chance they'll accept the invitation... that's not bad odds," Avery replies, trying to inject some optimism.

"I love your way of looking at things positively, Avery," Jordan says, a smile evident in his voice despite the delicate topic.

"You know, Jordan, sometimes it just takes a small gesture to mend old relationships. This could be the right opportunity to reconnect," Avery suggests gently.

"You're right, Avery. Maybe I should take this chance to try to rekindle the relationship. After all, such an important event in my life could be the perfect pretext for getting closer," Jordan reflects, considering the idea with renewed spirit.

"Exactly, and it doesn't matter how it goes. What's important is that you have no regrets for not trying. And who knows, maybe they'll be pleasantly surprised and proud to see how much you've grown, both as an artist and as a person," Avery encourages.

Avery had known the weight of emptiness, the deafening silence left by the loss of her parents, taken from life too soon. With them, she had a deep bond, a heart-to-heart affinity that went beyond mere blood relation, a relationship that time could never erode. Illness had first claimed her father, taking him away on a journey with no return, and then it was her mother's turn, consumed by grief and despair over the loss of her lifelong companion.

Jordan still had the privilege of having living parents, and Avery did not hesitate to urge him to cultivate and repair the bridges with his family.

"It's not wise to harbor resentment towards those who gave us life," Avery said with a voice imbued with pain transformed into wisdom.

"We are an extension of them, their blood flows in our veins, their DNA is the secret code that binds us to them, a vital and karmic energy that unites us across generations. Every time we get angry with our parents, it's as if we direct that same anger towards ourselves, attracting only negativity into our existence."

Avery insisted on this point with a passion that tempered the sadness in her eyes. "Even if they may have made mistakes in dealing with us, it's our duty to love them and allow them to follow their own destiny, without taking on burdens that don't belong to us. They have their own path to walk, just as we have ours. Life is too short and precious to waste on misunderstandings and regrets."

This was the advice Avery gave to Jordan, hoping he could find the strength to forgive and reconcile, before time made such a possibility an unattainable luxury.

"Alright, I'll take your advice. I'll send that invitation. Thank you, Avery, for encouraging me..." exclaims Jordan, already feeling a sense of relief.

"It's nothing, Jordan. I'm here for that. Now, let's move forward with the organization of the vernissage. We have a lot of work to do!" concludes Avery, ready to focus again on the project awaiting them.

The beach

"Dear Axel, I'm sorry for not responding to your messages right away, but I needed some space to reflect," Avery begins in her message. "I think that, for our own good, or at least for mine, it's better to take a break and not see each other for a while. I haven't fully processed the situation that has arisen between us. You know how much I value you and care about our friendship; that's precisely why I prefer to let some time pass. Right now, I feel torn between disappointment and anger, and I hate feeling these emotions. I will let you know when I feel ready to be myself again. Sending you a hug and please don't be mad at me."

Avery is well aware that a message cannot replace the clarity and immediacy of a phone call or, even better, a face-to-face conversation. However, in the emotional turmoil she finds herself in, writing was the only option that seemed manageable.

The moment Avery presses the send button, her gaze falls on a message notification from Lorraine: "Done. In a month, it will be official." A smile brushes her lips. "Finally some good news," she whispers to herself. She doesn't even have time to put down the phone when the sound of the intercom announces Eric's arrival.
"Come in," she responds, her voice veiled with a cold detachment. Deep down, she would have preferred to be anywhere but there. Eric's presence makes her nervous; even though he is no longer her husband, he still has that inexplicable power to unsettle her, to make her heart beat in her chest for all the wrong reasons.

With quick and decisive gestures, she hides the headset and webcam in the bedroom, determined not to give him any chance to interfere in her life again. "Hi Avery," he greets her. "Hi, you know where it is," Avery replies, tense as a violin string, pointing towards the studio.

"Relax. You should be happy, soon you won't have anything of mine in this house," says Eric, beginning to load the boxes onto a trolley. Avery chooses silence as her response, returning to her work on the computer placed on the living room table.

After a couple of hours, with the studio finally empty, Avery realizes how much more spacious the room now feels. Eric throws one last jab before leaving:
"Who's the lucky one?" She looks at him, surprised by the question.
"You're always so absent-minded. You left the wine glasses in the sink to wash," he observes.

"Mind your own business, Eric. It's none of your concern how I manage my things, let alone my dishes," replies Avery, irritation clearly audible in her voice.
"How dare you! Get out," she exclaims, her patience now exhausted.

"Wow, what a reaction. It's not like I accused you of a crime... Relax," he retorts. Each time Eric says "relax," Avery's irritation grows exponentially, unable to bear that word, especially when uttered by him.

"Hi Avery, I was wondering which place you'd prefer for our avatars to meet. Ah, and will you use your name for your avatar? So we can easily recognize each other... mine will be named Jordan, original, right? I've selected some scenarios I find interesting and would like your opinion on them. Here's the list:
Virtual Beaches: ideal places for walking together at sunset.
Virtual Cafes and Restaurants: where we can share intimate moments and enjoy live concerts or events.
Art Galleries and Museums: a great choice for those who love culture and want to explore virtual exhibitions together.
Parks and Gardens: perfect for peaceful conversations or admiring the beauty of virtual nature.

Arcades or Sporting Events: if you prefer something more active or competitive, these are ideal places.

Islands and Exotic Locations: for those looking for extraordinary settings for romantic adventures or shared explorations.

Let me know what you think!

Best regards,
Jordan"

"Finally, I have a space all to myself," Avery exclaims, setting up the studio with great attention to detail.

"There's an ideal spot for the PC and all the privacy I need," she adds, while setting up the webcam and browsing through her emails, noticing Jordan's message.

"It's odd that he didn't just send a simple message," she reflects, but reading the email makes her understand why.

"Wow, so many choices for environments, I'd like to explore them all," Avery thinks, also contemplating what name to give her avatar.

"Avy would be perfect, it was the nickname my father used when I was little. I like it."

For our first meeting, the idea of a deserted beach full of palms and shells, where we can walk and listen to the sound of the sea, fascinates me, Avery reflects.

"It's incredible what can be done with technology," she says, preparing to respond to Jordan.

"Dear Jordan,

After reflecting on your list of evocative environments, I've decided that the idea of meeting on a deserted beach, surrounded by palm trees and shells, with the gentle sound of the sea in the background, is simply perfect. It seems like the ideal place for our first virtual meeting. How about connecting in a couple of hours? That would be the perfect time for me.

Also, I've chosen the name for my avatar: it will be 'Avy,' a name very dear to me that brings back sweet childhood memories. I hope you like it and that it helps you easily recognize me in our virtual world.

I'm looking forward to exploring the deserted island together and spending time in your company. Let me know if the time I proposed works for you as well.

See you soon,

Avery (Avy)"

"Dear Avery,

Perfect, I'm glad you chose that destination. I wanted to let you know that the platform we will be using supports voice chat, so we'll have the opportunity to talk directly using microphones. This feature is highly appreciated for how it makes communication more direct and natural, greatly enriching the meeting experience. Of course, if you prefer or if needed, text chat will remain available at all times…

I've arranged everything to ensure a private and intimate setting where we can talk and walk without interruptions.

As it is a private environment, you will need my invitation which you must accept.
Here are the details you need to access:

Log in to the platform and navigate to the section for private environments.
Search for the environment named "Virtual Deserted Beach".
When prompted, enter the provided access code.
Once inside, you will find yourself directly on our private beach. I was thinking we could meet at 9 PM. What do you say?
I recommend logging in a few minutes before the scheduled time, so you have time to get accustomed. If you encounter any difficulties, do not hesitate to contact me.

I look forward to meeting you in this little virtual paradise we have chosen. It will be an unforgettable experience, I'm sure.

See you later, dear Avy.

A kiss, Jordan"

As soon as Avery finishes reading Jordan's email, she begins to feel an unusual excitement: the idea of a virtual meeting makes her both nervous and thrilled. She wonders how Lorraine would react if she knew about all this. Lorraine, who doesn't even own a smartphone and persists in using an outdated mobile phone. She despises emoticons, videos, reels, considers memes foolish, and is deeply skeptical of technology. Whenever the conversation turns to technology with Avery, Lorraine never misses a chance to repeat her mantra: "Snowden docet!"

As Avery tidies up the kitchen, she realizes that their meeting time is approaching. She hasn't prepared anything to eat, preferring to order Thai food; she is particularly fond of rice with vegetables. While putting the two glasses back in the china cabinet, her thoughts unintentionally drift to Axel, recalling intimate moments...

"No, no, no... not now," she scolds herself, trying to maintain calm and serenity. "I don't want to ruin this evening." Then, she reflects on how Eric immediately noticed those glasses: all because of his passion for wines.

As an expert sommelier, he had an impressive collection at home: white wine glasses with narrow openings to emphasize the aromas, those with wider openings for structured wines, the balloon glass for prestigious reds, champagne flutes in at least three varieties, and finally the tulip glasses for sweet and fortified wines...
"I should have put away those two glasses immediately," Avery thinks, bringing her mind back to the present.

The clock shows 20:40, and Jordan is getting ready for their virtual date. After moving a small bookcase, he has found the necessary space to set up his gaming corner. This time, however, it's not about the usual hours spent playing and leveling up; tonight's challenge is different but no less thrilling. Even for him, a veteran of the web, this is the first time he is interacting so directly with another person, or to be precise, with an avatar. And the feeling is strangely intense...

"Now I'll send the invitation to Avery and then wait for her to connect," Jordan thinks, sending the message.

Both enter their login credentials on the selected platform, which takes them directly to the virtual environment prepared for the occasion.
Using the invitation and code provided by Jordan, Avery accesses the reserved environment. Jordan, already connected, waits for her arrival.

Their avatars recognize each other immediately. Avery has chosen "Avy" as the name for her avatar, while Jordan uses his usual pseudonym. The appearance of the avatars reflects the personal preferences they selected during profile creation on the platform.

Avery's avatar doesn't look much like her real self: medium build, with red hair, large eyes, and olive skin. For the occasion, she has chosen a light dress and sandals, and wears a large hat, adding a further touch of personality.

Jordan's avatar is completely different from his physical likeness, with distinctive features such as a beard, dark hair, and fair skin. He also wears a comfortable beach outfit for their virtual date.

"Hi Avery, welcome! I'm so glad you're here."

"Hi Jordan! This place is incredible; I can't wait to explore it with you."

"Yes, a beach at sunset is perfect for our first meeting. What do you think?"

"It's wonderful, really beyond my expectations. And that virtual sunset is so realistic!"

They walk in silence for a moment, letting the sound of the virtual waves fill the space between them.

Avery, bending down to "pick up" a virtual shell:
"Look at this, Jordan! They seem so real. It's incredible what we can do in these worlds."

"Yes, the metaverse offers us endless possibilities. I like to think of it as a bit like building our own dreams."

They "sit" on some rocks, overlooking the digital sea.

"You know, I never imagined feeling so... connected, in a place like this. It's strange, but in a good way."

"I understand completely. It's a new feeling for me too. It makes me reflect on how intense and profound our virtual interactions can be..."

"Exactly. And talking to you here, now, makes me feel as if we're not really that far apart."

"I'm glad to hear that, Avery. And I hope this is just the beginning of many more adventures here together."

Sharing a moment of silence, both are lost in admiration of the virtual landscape, aware that they have started something unique and special.

As their avatars continue to walk along the virtual beach, a curious sparkle in the "eyes" of Avery's digital self catches Jordan's attention, prompting him to delve into a topic that has been on his mind for a while.

"Avy, I'm curious," Jordan begins playfully, "how much do you really resemble your avatar? I tried to be as true to my real appearance as possible," Jordan lies.

Avery bursts into light, melodious laughter, resonating through the voice chat.
"Oh, Jordan, if only you could see me! I'm quite different from my avatar. I wanted to experiment with a look I normally wouldn't have, you know? That's the beauty of the metaverse, I can be whoever I want to be."

Jordan laughs along with her, admiring her openness.

"That's fantastic! I love that you can explore different aspects of yourself here. I must admit, the idea of experimenting never occurred to me. I'm pretty much the digital version of myself, with the same hair, the same eyes... Although, well, maybe here I'm a bit more in shape!" he continues to lie.

"That's what makes these spaces so special," Avery responds, her avatar casting a knowing glance at Jordan's.

"We can be true to ourselves in ways we can't imagine in the real world, or decide to explore a completely new part of us. And by the way, I find your choice to remain true to your appearance just as fascinating. It shows you're comfortable with who you are."

"Well, thanks, Avy," says Jordan, a bit embarrassed but clearly flattered.
"But now that you mention it, I might start experimenting a bit more with my avatar. Maybe in our next meeting, you might not recognize me!"

"You know, Jordan," Avery begins, her voice filtered through the microphone conveying a sense of wonder.
"It always amazes me how capable avatars are in these spaces. The fact that they can walk, run, sit, and even make hand gestures... it's incredible."

Jordan nods, though Avery can only see it through the action of his avatar. "And that's not all," she continues, "they can interact with the environment around them, pick up objects, use virtual equipment or tools, and even dance. It makes me feel as if the possibilities here are truly endless."

Avery's comment prompts Jordan to reflect on the scope of virtual worlds, which go beyond mere meeting places. These spaces allow for overcoming the physical limitations of the real world, offering the freedom to express oneself in more inventive and personal ways. Although aware that lying does not fall under creativity, in this instance, he does not feel guilty.

After spending enjoyable time together, they agree that this virtual experience has exceeded their expectations and decide to plan another meeting.

The encounter in the metaverse between Jordan and Avery becomes a significant memory for both, a first step towards a connection that transcends the boundary between virtual and real.

Reflections

After their first online meeting, Avery finds herself submerged in an ocean of thoughts. Sitting in front of her computer, still connected to the now deserted digital platform, she lets her thoughts roam unbounded, trying to make sense of what she has just experienced.

For Avery, the encounter with Jordan in the metaverse was an experience that exceeded all expectations. The ability to walk together on a virtual beach, to exchange silences and laughter as if they were physically present, opened her eyes to the depth and meaning that connections made in virtual spaces can achieve.

She reflects on how, in this alternate universe, the restrictions of the real world seem to dissolve, granting a freedom of expression without equal. Avery is surprised by how easy it was to open up to Jordan, how the words flowed naturally, perhaps aided by the safe distance their avatars provided. This distance, instead of being a barrier, became a bridge that facilitated authentic and sincere dialogue.

She also thinks about her choice of avatar, "Avy," and how it allowed her to explore aspects of herself that she might not have had the courage to show in reality. The freedom to be whoever she wants, to change her appearance at will, provided her with a range of possibilities to express her identity in new ways.

However, Avery wonders how much of their interaction was influenced by the virtual nature of their meeting. She questions whether the connection felt with Jordan would have been the same in person, without a screen between them. This reflection leads her to contemplate the value of relationships in the metaverse compared to those in the physical world.

Despite these doubts, she concludes that the virtual experience with Jordan was a valuable step towards understanding herself and others. She realizes that, regardless of the means through which people connect, what matters is the authenticity of the shared feelings and the willingness to explore new realms of human existence together.

With a smile on her face and a feeling of gratitude in her heart, Avery logs off, eager to discover where this new path of virtual connections and personal discoveries will lead her.

Jordan is left alone, the glow of the screen illuminating the contours of his room, reflecting on what has just happened. His encounter with Avery in the metaverse has left an indelible mark, but with it, also a burden that now seems to weigh on his shoulders with suffocating intensity. The lies told about his appearance begin to weigh heavily on his conscience, triggering a storm of reflections and doubts.

The ease with which he had chosen to alter reality in the virtual world now catches him by surprise. Jordan had imagined that, in that digital context, physical appearance would not matter, convincing himself that it was permissible to reinvent himself. Yet, now he realizes that every word, every unauthentic description of himself, could be an obstacle to the true connection that has begun to form with Avery.

He reflects on how the freedom offered by the metaverse can be a double-edged sword: on one hand, it allows for the exploration of otherwise unexplored or suppressed identities and self-expressions due to social expectations; on the other hand, it hides the risk of building relationships on foundations that are not completely solid, based on idealized and, to some extent, unreal versions of oneself.

The thought of having to confront Avery with the truth disturbs him. Jordan fears that revealing the reality behind the avatar could not only jeopardize their burgeoning connection but also expose him to judgment for having concealed the truth. This fear is heightened by the fact that the sincerity and authenticity of the moments shared in the metaverse have been for him a deeply liberating and genuine experience.

However, beyond the apprehensions, Jordan begins to understand the intrinsic value of honesty and vulnerability in human relationships. He realizes that, as tempting as it may be to present oneself in the way one wishes to be seen, authentic relationships require a foundation of sincerity and transparency, even at the risk of revealing one's insecurities.

This moment of introspection leads him to consider that perhaps true courage lies in showing oneself for who one really is, accepting the risk of being vulnerable. Jordan starts to contemplate the possibility of opening up to Avery, hoping that the strength of the bond created can overcome the barriers erected by his initial lies.

With a mix of fear and hope, Jordan decides that the next time he connects with Avery, he will try to find the courage to be authentic. He mentally prepares for how to approach the conversation, planning to reveal the truth as if it were a trivial joke, made in a moment of light-heartedness, with the conviction that it would not hurt anyone.

In his mind, he carefully crafts his words, trying to strike the right balance between apologizing for his mistake and the hope of keeping the connection with Avery intact. "Avery," he will start, "what I'm about to tell you might surprise you. When we met, I chose to present myself in a way... not entirely accurate. I wanted to impress you, perhaps. I thought it was just a small joke, something insignificant that wouldn't affect what we are to each other."

Jordan imagines continuing, explaining how, in the metaverse, the temptation to alter one's image can seem harmless, almost like wearing a costume at a party.
"But I've realized," he will say, "that even the smallest disguise can create a distance between us, a barrier to the sincerity we both deserve."

He hopes that by presenting his choice as a lapse in judgment born from playful intent, he can mitigate Avery's disappointment and maybe even coax a smile from her. "I didn't want to deceive you," he will insist, "I just wanted to create a moment, an unforgettable experience between us. But now I understand that the most meaningful experiences are those built on truth."

Jordan clings to the hope that this explanation will pave the way for a deeper dialogue, where both can share their fears, their desires, and, most importantly, their truths. He imagines concluding with an expression of vulnerability,
"Avery, I really care about what we have. I hope we can get past this, that you can understand … I want our bond to be based on who we truly are, beyond any joke and any avatar."

With this plan in mind, Jordan begins to write the message to Avery, hoping that his attempt to correct the course can not only save their relationship but also make it stronger through renewed sincerity and trust. However, he decides not to send it immediately, leaving the email open with the cursor blinking...

"Here... if I hadn't made that mess," Avery reflects, "I would probably be on the phone with Axel right now, talking about the absurdity of this online evening. Instead, here I am alone, unable to share what I feel with anyone else.

I already know Lorraine would call me crazy, saying we resemble zombies tethered to a cable, perpetually seeking an alternative existence, unable to tolerate our own essence, tied to cables, headsets, and joysticks. Irresistibly drawn to the couch, we find ourselves mesmerized by animated figures dancing before our eyes. Perhaps it's the weight of a mediocre identity that drives us toward an escape into an unreal and almost ghostly dimension... it would have been better if I had just gone to sleep...

It's curious how I can know so many people and yet feel, despite everything, so isolated," Avery muses.

"Maybe that's also why I threw myself so impulsively into this thing with Jordan: have I really reached such a level of desperation? Okay, Avery, stop brooding, it's time to go to sleep... at least I should manage a couple of hours," she thinks as she settles under the covers.

Despite having slept little, the following morning she is surprisingly full of energy. She arrives at the office on time and gets straight to work without delay. Lunch break comes unexpectedly, and immersed in her work, she decides to skip it. Her day is marked by an unusual hyperactivity and almost feverish haste. As soon as she finishes the last call, she hurries back home, quickly eats some fruit, and positions herself in front of the computer.

"Maybe we can connect a bit earlier tonight," she types, addressing Jordan, "so we don't end up finishing too late. You know, I still have a pretty demanding routine. Is that okay with you? See you later. Kisses, Avy."

Jordan's dream

Jordan logs onto the virtual platform, his heart racing, aware of the weight of the words he is about to utter. Avery appears on the screen, her avatar smiling as always, but her virtual eyes seem to search for something, perhaps a hint of what is to come.

"Hey Avery," Jordan begins with an uncertain voice, "there's something important I need to tell you. It's about our first meeting and... well, how I presented myself to you."

Avery listens, her virtual expression impassive, urging him with a nod to continue. Jordan then dives in, repeating almost exactly the words he had planned. He explains the joke concept, downplaying the deceit as a poorly considered choice to make their meeting more interesting. He emphasizes that he had no malicious intentions and that his priority was to create a meaningful connection, despite the not entirely truthful premises.

Throughout his speech, Avery remains silent, listening intently. Her avatar betrays no emotions, but it is clear that she is pondering each word.

"I understand why you might have done it," Avery finally responds, her voice calm yet filled with emotion.
"The metaverse gives us the chance to be whoever we want, and I can imagine that the temptation to alter some truths about ourselves is strong. But...," she pauses, searching for the right words, "honesty is important, Jordan. For me, trust is fundamental, especially in a place where everything can be questioned."

Jordan listens, feeling a mix of relief and fear for Avery's reaction.

"I'm sorry, Avery. Really. I didn't want to jeopardize what we're building. I promise that from now on, I'll be completely honest. Our connection means too much to me."

Avery smiles slightly, as a strange hissing noise begins...a continuous and annoying sound...beep...beep

Jordan is wrapped in a fog of confusion, unable to discern whether he is still immersed in dreams or awake. It is the unmistakable melody of his phone that pulls him out of the uncertain reality...

He was not online with Avery and had confessed nothing. "Too good to be true," he says to himself, feeling that everything was so vivid it seemed real. As he heads to the bathroom, he reflects on the dream, considering it perhaps a positive sign: in the dream, Avery had been understanding. "Come on, Jordan," he encourages himself, trying to draw courage from the nocturnal illusion.

Jordan settles at his work station, aware that he's a bit behind on some projects, with deadlines looming dangerously close. After re-reading the email he prepared for Avery, he chooses not to send it.
"It's better to talk to her directly at our next online meeting," he promises himself, thinking about which private virtual space to choose for their next encounter. The idea of an art gallery flashes through his mind, evoking memories of their early exchanges.
"A great idea," he convinces himself, imagining how that setting could be the perfect backdrop for their conversation.

Wow, Avery is already free and would like to connect earlier...
"Ok, I think I can do that," Jordan thinks. He types quickly:
"Hi Avery, that's perfect for me. I'll send the invite within half an hour and see you online. I've prepared a surprise for you, hope you'll like it. A kiss, J."

Meanwhile, Avery enjoys choosing a new look for her avatar: not sure of the setting Jordan will have in mind, she opts for something comfortable, shorts and a T-shirt, leaving aside the hat, but keeping her red hair in a lively ponytail.

"I look like a schoolgirl," she reflects, a bit uncertain, but then reassures herself thinking that there's no need to take it too seriously.

"Wow, this place is incredible!" exclaims Avery, spinning her avatar to admire every detail of the virtual gallery.
"You've really outdone yourself this time, Jordan."

Jordan has set up an environment reminiscent of an art gallery, with walls adorned with digital paintings that seem almost to come to life thanks to their vividness of colors and the three-dimensionality of the effects.

Jordan smiles, pleased that the surprise has been well received.

"I'm glad you like it. I thought it would be nice to recreate the kind of environment that marked our first meetings here in the metaverse," he replies, guiding her through the gallery.

They walk virtually side by side, commenting on the displayed artworks. Each painting becomes a pretext to share thoughts and reflections, bringing them even closer. The conversation flows naturally, with laughter and deeper moments of reflection.

After a while, Jordan slows down, as if searching for the right moment to shift the conversation's tone. Avery notices and, curious, encourages him to go on.
"Is something wrong, Jordan?" she asks.

"I wanted to talk to you about my avatar," Jordan begins, his voice filled with hesitation. Avery looks at him intently, sensing the seriousness of the moment. But then, seeing Avery's open and curious expression, Jordan changes his mind.

"But, you know, there's something else more important I'd like to talk to you about," he continues, deviating from his original plan.

With a pause full of anticipation, Jordan launches his new proposal, trying to create an even more significant moment between them.

"Avery, how would you feel about experiencing something more... intimate? A meeting just for the two of us, something that could bring us even closer on a personal level."

Jordan's proposal takes Avery by surprise. A virtual couple's meeting, designed to explore their connection in a private and intimate space, is a leap from their previous interactions. This idea introduces a level of closeness and vulnerability that Avery had not yet considered in their virtual relationship.

"Do you mean... something more personal?" Avery asks, trying to fully grasp the implications of what Jordan is suggesting.

"Yes, exactly," Jordan confirms.

"I think it could be a way for us to get to know each other even better, in a more private context and, in a sense, more real."

Avery ponders the proposal, feeling a mix of excitement and nervousness. The idea of such an intimate meeting in the metaverse challenges the boundaries of their relationship, leading them towards a new dimension of virtual intimacy.

After a moment of reflection, Avery responds

"Jordan, I realize this could really change things between us. And... I agree. I'm curious to explore this new dimension with you."

The decision to proceed with a virtual couple's meeting marks a turning point in their relationship, opening doors to a level of connection and mutual understanding never experienced before. Both are aware that they are about to venture into uncharted territories, but the prospect of discovering new aspects of their connection fills them with palpable anticipation.

As their second virtual link-up in the art gallery comes to an end, Avery and Jordan are deeply aware of how the expectations for their future together are changing, rising to new and bold directions. The proposal of an intimate virtual meeting has introduced a completely new dynamic, marking a point of no return towards greater closeness and complicity.

"So, we'll see each other soon for... our special date," says Jordan, his voice laden with emotion reflecting the significance of what they have decided to undertake. There is a mix of excitement and nervousness in the air, a palpable sense of anticipation for what is to come.

"Yes, I can't wait," responds Avery, with a smile that manages to shine through even the digitality of her avatar.
"I realize that we are about to explore something very personal, and that makes me... happy, but also a bit anxious."

Both share a moment of silence, reflecting on how quickly their relationship is evolving and how each decision now seems to carry greater weight, a promise of intimacy and mutual discovery that neither of them had fully anticipated.

"This will bring us closer in ways we probably can't even imagine right now," adds Jordan, trying to reassure Avery as well as himself.

"But I am convinced that, whatever happens, it will be an enriching experience for both of us."

Avery nods, feeling encouraged by Jordan's words. "You're right. It's a bold step, but I'm happy we're taking it together. I feel that this will lead us to understand aspects of each other that we would never have discovered otherwise."

With these words, they say goodbye, leaving behind the virtual gallery but taking with them the promise of a future meeting that promises to be unlike anything they have experienced so far.

As they disconnect, both reflect on the deep significance of what they have decided to explore, aware that the bar of expectations is being raised and that the choices they are making are taking a decidedly unique turn, marking a new chapter in their virtual story.

One Step Beyond

"How does an intimate meeting occur in the metaverse?" Avery finds herself typing into her smartphone the next day as she goes to work. She is completely unfamiliar with that world and what she agreed to the previous evening, caught up in the emotion and Jordan's convincing voice.

An intimate meeting in the metaverse takes place in a private and personalized virtual space, created to facilitate a shared experience between two people wishing to explore a deeper and more personal level of connection. This type of meeting is made possible by the advancement of immersive technologies, such as virtual reality (VR), which allow users to interact in three-dimensional digital environments. Emerging technologies can add elements like virtual touch, where wearable devices transmit tactile sensations, further enriching the shared experience.

Avery wonders, "Did Jordan perhaps imagine something like this for our meeting?" as she continues her online research to delve deeper into the subject. Her curiosity leads her to discover haptic suits... *advanced garments that, along with coordinated pants, are capable of conveying realistic tactile sensations to the user, simulated based on events occurring within a virtual environment managed by software or video games. These haptic suits, with their tactile feedback systems, have the extraordinary ability to transform digital signals into sensory experiences that mimic real physical contact, such as caresses, vibrations, pushes, or even more intense impacts.*

"Okay, I'll buy one; why not try?" Avery convinces herself. "After all, I can afford this expense: it's been over a year since I last indulged in the luxury of a vacation, so I might as well seek some escape from the daily routine with just a click," she reflects while finalizing the online purchase. "And I'll add the haptic glove too," she decides, reading the description carefully. *The haptic glove, derived from the Greek 'hapto' meaning touch, is a wearable device that not only tracks the movement of the fingers in a virtual environment but also simulates the tactile sensations one would feel when touching a real object. This simulation occurs through interaction with the DreamLens viewer, which recognizes the virtual object. The glove is capable of providing realistic tactile feedback down to the fingertips, inducing in the brain a perception of contact that, although not real, is interpreted as authentic due to the virtual interaction with the object.*

Meanwhile, Jordan starts to seriously consider an alternative plan. He feels the need to leave behind his life in a city that now seems too alien to him, finding nothing left that ties him to that place. There is also the fear that Ethan might reappear at any moment, and Jordan knows he lacks the determination to definitively reject him. In addition, the prospect of future exposure, Avery's support, and his own talent could open unexpected doors for him anywhere in the world he decides to move.

Avery is a highly influential figure, and for Jordan, it was not difficult to find out where she lives, the circles she moves in, and he already knows what she looks like physically. He has chosen not to reveal any of this research to her, appreciating Avery's genuine spontaneity and the sense of security she feels in interacting behind the screen. However, Jordan can't help but think that she has been a bit too naive in believing that her identity was completely secure.

Jordan begins to seriously consider the idea of moving to New York, seeing his future there. Despite never having lived in the United States, he feels partly American. His grandmother Lynette came from a small Midwestern town. She fell in love with an airline pilot and traveled the world, eventually choosing to settle in Europe. Her children, including Milia, Jordan's mother, were all born in Europe. Milia had explored various European cities, taking advantage of programs like Erasmus and various scholarships; she was a true genius and had inherited her mother's adventurous spirit. On one of her trips, she met Danel, Jordan's father, of Basque origin, and it was there they decided to settle down and start a family in the Basque Country, a region in northern Spain known as Euskadi, comprising the provinces of Álava, Biscay, and Gipuzkoa.

Jordan felt suffocated in the same country where he was born and raised, where his parents continued to live. He had inherited his grandmother's nomadic spirit: for him, no place was truly home, and at the same time, every place could be. He deeply felt that it was time to seek new horizons, convinced that meeting new people and exploring different environments would positively affect his mental health and creative streak.

While Jordan was absorbed in his thoughts about the future, Avery was carried away by excitement for their upcoming virtual meeting. It was Jordan's task to choose a romantic setting for the date, and Avery was ready to contribute with her personal touch. Her daydream was interrupted by the sudden ringing of the phone. "Hello, Axel," she answered, surprised.

"Hey Avery," he said, his voice tinged with a hint of embarrassment.
"I know you asked me to wait, but I can't. I need to clear things up with you. I'm not okay with what's happening between us..."

Avery listened in silence, unable to formulate a ready response, when Axel revealed he was right below her house. Avery found herself torn by conflicting emotions: on one hand, she ardently wished things with Axel could go back to how they were before; on the other, she was aware that, at least for the moment, this would not be possible, and that she would have to keep her distance.

"Come on up," she finally said, giving in.

"I'm sorry, Avery, for showing up unexpectedly. It's not like me to act so impulsively, but I must confess that since that evening, I can't find sleep anymore. I'm losing focus at work, and I'm not interested in food... I'm restless," confesses Axel, still standing in front of the door. With a tone of genuine concern, Avery replies,

"I'm sorry to hear you feel this way. I too think back to what happened, but I'm trying to divert my thoughts from that, and I think you should do the same. But please, come in, don't just stand there at the door."

"I can't take lightly what happened between us. I've had many relationships in my life, as you well know, some serious and others fleeting, and I've always managed to balance passion and reason. But this time it's different, Avery... I don't know how you managed to shake me up so deeply."

Avery realizes that Axel's words don't strike her deeply. Her best friend is in pieces, claims to be in love with her, and after giving in to a night of passion, now tries to convince her of his unprecedented love.

"I don't know what to say," Avery expresses, the only genuine feeling she can muster at the moment.

"I can't do anything but tell you I'm sorry; I don't know what you expect from me. But one thing is clear: what happened must not happen again. I can listen to you all afternoon if that makes you feel better..."

Axel realizes that maybe it was a mistake to come to her. What was he hoping for? That Avery, moved by compassion, would welcome him with open arms?

"You're right, Avery, perhaps I had unrealistic expectations of you. It's better that I leave..." he says, heading towards the door. Just then, he runs into Eric, who was about to ring the doorbell.

"Axel?" exclaims Eric, surprised and noticing his agitation. "Hi, Eric," responds Axel, trying in vain to maintain a feigned calm.

"Eric, what are you doing here? Couldn't you have sent a message or called?" Avery interjects.

"I sent you a message, if you didn't read it, that's not my fault... I had written that I would come by to pick up a folder of documents I left in your desk drawer," says Eric, entering without waiting for permission and immediately sensing that something must have happened between Avery and Axel.

Eric bursts into laughter without restraint.

"Ah, no, tell me it's not true... it's obvious from a mile away... you were the famous drinking buddy from the other night, right Axel?" With a mix of irritation and embarrassment, Avery intervenes:

"Enough, Eric, take what you need and leave, please." However, Eric doesn't listen and, turning to Axel again, teases:

"Hey, buddy, you finally made it with her, huh? It took you thirty years, but, you know, better late than never, hahaha!" Eric laughs openly in front of a silent Axel, who doesn't know what to say.

"How long have you been chasing her? Since university? And you weren't even that good at hiding it, if even I noticed," continues Eric, oblivious to the growing embarrassment. Axel casts a glance at Avery but remains speechless.

"See, the silence is almost a confirmation," adds Eric with a note of sarcasm in his voice.
"But be careful, my friend. Avery can be quite unpredictable: today she might be crazy about you, and tomorrow already interested in someone else."

Axel, feeling provoked by Eric's words and wanting to defend Avery, reacts with a burst of energy uncharacteristic for him. With a quick and decisive move, he pushes Eric against the wall, pinning one arm behind his back. Without saying a word, he drags him to the study, makes him grab the documents he had come to get, and, maintaining a firm grip, pushes him out of the house.
"I could really hurt you, Eric," Axel threatens with a stern tone, giving a final shove. "You better leave, so no one gets hurt."

Finally, Eric stops with his sarcastic laughter, leaving Avery in a silence heavy with tension. She remains motionless, phone still in hand, reflecting on what just happened. Axel's unexpected defense leaves her surprised and, in some way, helps her understand the depth of his feelings, despite the complexity of their situation.

"I'm sorry Avery, forgive me for everything," says Axel, quickly walking away without waiting for a response. Meanwhile, Avery's phone beeps, announcing a new message from Jordan:
"Dear Avery, I've found the perfect place for our meeting: I'll send you the invitation, see you soon. A kiss."

"What timing, Jordan," thinks Avery, still disturbed by the recent events between Axel and Eric.

Trying to divert her mind from what just happened, she sits in front of the computer, determined to modify her avatar again. By now, the meetings with Jordan have the great power to draw her like a magnet to the PC screen...they take priority over everything else…

Meanwhile, Jordan had spent time searching for virtual settings, looking for that ideal place that could combine intimacy and comfort. After considering various options, he had settled on a cozy mountain retreat, equipped with a spectacular panoramic view of the starry sky, perfect for creating an intimate and romantic atmosphere. Before initiating the connection, Jordan carefully reviewed the virtual environment, ensuring that every detail contributed to making the space as welcoming and perfect as possible. Virtual candles cast a soft light, and a carefully selected playlist provided a background, adding an extra note of intimacy to the atmosphere.

Avery, for her part, took a moment to reflect before connecting, taking some deep breaths to ease the excitement and apprehension. She wanted to enter this virtual meeting ready to openly receive and share emotions, open to the infinite possibilities their conversation might offer.
When they finally connect, the energy between them is palpable, even through the screen. They greet each other with a mix of shyness and excitement, ready to explore this new dimension of their relationship. The evening promises to be a significant journey in their connection, a bold but desired step towards a deeper and more intimate understanding of what brings them together.

Avery wanted Avy to appear sensual yet discreet, so she had dressed her in an elegant black dress that gracefully accentuated the curves, unlike her less pronounced ones, paired with a pair of refined stiletto heels and leaving her hair flowing over her shoulders.
"Avy, you look stunning," Jordan remarks.
"Thank you, Jordan. This place is enchanting, and the music? Was it your choice?" asks Avery.

"Yes, Avery. I've selected romantic tracks ranging from the '80s to the present, hoping to match your tastes..." he responds, as their avatars draw closer and Jordan gently takes Avy's hands.

In that digital yet incredibly intimate atmosphere, Jordan brings his avatar closer to Avy's, initiating a courtship of carefully chosen words meant to touch Avery's heart.

"Avy, you are the brightest star in this virtual sky. Being here with you, at this moment, makes me forget that the outside world exists."

"Jordan, your words wrap around me like a hug... I never thought a virtual meeting could feel so... real."

Under the soft light of the virtual candles, the avatars begin to dance slowly, moving in harmony with the romantic notes of the playlist. The music of the moment seems to exist just for them, a perfect backdrop for a dance that needs no words.

"Avery, every movement with you is a step into a dream from which I don't want to wake. I wish I could hold you like this forever, feel the beat of your heart close to mine, even if only in this virtual world."

As they dance, Jordan, encouraged by the intensity of the moment, goes further, daring to express deeper desires. He finds boldness in the distance provided by the screen and begins to court Avery, whispering first in a romantic manner, then more assertively, uttering phrases designed to arouse her desire.
"Avery, how would you feel about experimenting with a 'physical contact' simulation at our next connection using the haptic gloves and suits? There are so many things I'd like to do with you. I wish I could hold you in my arms, in an embrace we can feel with every fiber of our being."

Avery receives the proposal with a mix of shyness and surprise, but in her heart, she was already prepared to embrace it all.

"Jordan... this place, created from our dreams, makes me wish there was a way to make all this more tangible." Avery is truly driven by an intense curiosity to discover these new worlds in every aspect. She feels like a teenager experiencing her first crush: everything seems fascinating and shrouded in an aura of mystery.

Meanwhile, the avatars continue to dance, wrapped in romantic melodies, while Jordan and Avery share a moment of deep virtual connection, suspended between desire and reality, exploring the boundaries of an affection that seems to transcend the digital.

Blurred boundaries

Jordan has that special gift of making me feel good, with his ability to make every other thought fade away... I feel ready to dare more, he's right, it's time to move forward. With the haptic suits, we could really feel each other's presence, touch each other, and intensify the experience of our meetings. Avery reflects, browsing through the brochures for the vernissage that the designer sent her.

"Today my purchases should finally arrive," she muses. "So, maybe as early as tonight, I can test the suit and the glove..." and she finds herself feeling the excitement of a child waiting to unwrap presents on Christmas morning.

Her hopes are not dashed: arriving home, Avery quickly opens the packages and snaps a photo that she immediately sends to Jordan, accompanied by an intriguing message:

"Look what arrived... Shall we test it together?"

"Wow, Avery, you really know how to live... So, Murray Street... And what about the view? The Empire State Building, the Chrysler, the Brooklyn Bridge, Hudson Yards, Central Park, and then there's the Hudson and East River..." reflects Jordan, after managing to discover Avery's address.

"For someone who lives in such a place, you are surprisingly down-to-earth," he thinks. "But in the end, it seems you need me to feel truly alive. We will do many wonderful things together, sooner than you might think, dear Avery." He is already imagining meeting her in person, and now that he knows more about Avery's living context, Jordan is even more determined to become part of it. He has sensed her vulnerability and probably a sense of loneliness; he knows he just needs to overcome her resistance to transitioning from virtual to real, so he must be particularly persuasive. The photo sent by Avery comes as an encouraging signal. "You've really thought of everything," he reflects, before responding enthusiastically,
"Of course, my dear, I can't wait."

While he dreams of living in Manhattan's penthouses, Jordan finds himself having to look for a studio apartment to move into as soon as possible. He has already sent the termination letter for his small apartment; it will take at least three months to organize the move.

Meanwhile, Avery is completely unaware of Jordan's thoughts and finds herself grappling with the instructions to set up the haptic suit to her PC, a task that is proving to be more complicated than expected.

As the days and "meetings" passed, the use of the glove and haptic suits became for Avery and Jordan a form of addiction hard to break. Feeling each other's touch on the skin and the direct explicitness of their words left little room for imagination.
The introduction of the suits and glove had marked a decisive turning point in their relationship; the realistic sensation of touch had revolutionized the way they interacted. In the privacy of their virtual corner, they had indulged in gestures of intimacy, embraces, establishing an almost physical contact.

At the end of each session, Avery and Jordan needed a moment to regain awareness of reality, wondering if what they had experienced was tangible or still belonged to the realm of the virtual.

The daily dynamic between Avery and Jordan had taken an unprecedented direction: he would send the invitation, and together they would explore the metaverse for hours. They confided in each other, shared dreams and aspirations, and experienced moments of genuine intimacy. Avery found herself increasingly prolonging her time in front of the screen; after finishing work, she wanted nothing else. She had reduced her outings, especially in the evening, longing for the moment to return home and connect with Jordan. Her existence unfolded as if she were engaged in a real relationship, almost neglecting that her feelings had sprung solely from a charming voice and nothing more.

Jordan, convinced that Avery was now deeply involved in their story, feels it might be the right time to make her a new proposal.

It's dawn, and Jordan does something unusual: he calls Avery. Usually, they limit themselves to exchanging brief morning messages before dedicating themselves to their respective days. However, for Jordan, the time has come to make the decisive move.

Jordan's proposal

"Avery, these weeks with you have been incredible. Every meeting makes me feel closer to you, even though we are just in the metaverse," he begins, with a tone of voice that conveys sincerity. Avery listens carefully, sensing the intensity of the moment.

"So, this got me thinking... What would you say if we tried to take our connection outside of this virtual space? I would like to meet you in person, Avery," proposes Jordan, with a mix of hope and nervousness.

Avery is taken aback, Jordan's words echoing in her ears. The idea of turning their virtual connection into something tangible excites but also frightens her. "Jordan, this is a proposal I had never considered...," she responds after a brief silence, her heart racing.

"I know it's a big step, and I don't want to pressure you. Just, I feel that there's something special between us, and I would like to explore it beyond the screen," continues Jordan, trying to convey his desire without overwhelming Avery.

Avery ponders for a moment, weighing the possibilities and implications of such a meeting.
"Jordan, the idea scares me a bit, I won't lie. But... but I also would like to see you in person. I don't know if it can be the right next step for us... but we could give it a try... without burdening it with expectations..." she replies, still conflicted.

"Finally, Avery," pleased with having persuaded her, "it's time to elevate our story to a new level."

Jordan, who had meticulously planned his permanent move to New York, keeping it a secret from Avery, has already been in the city for two weeks.

Curiously, despite the months spent together, she had never asked him in which city he lived; they had discussed every possible topic, but Avery had always avoided that specific question. Now, however, it is necessary to start discussing concrete places, even though Jordan intends to reveal his true situation only after their first face-to-face meeting.

"This is really a fantastic opportunity for us, Avery, I honestly didn't dare hope for it... if you trust me, I'll arrange our meeting, but it won't be through a screen anymore. Finally, I'll be able to truly embrace you."

Avery struggles to believe that all this is really happening; she wants to shout her joy to the whole world. It's common for lovers to want to announce their love to everyone, but she realizes it might seem foolish to have to explain the details, like...
"It's wonderful that your boyfriend is coming to New York, but where did you meet?" And answering "Actually, we've never met in person, our relationship started in the metaverse" would leave the interlocutor speechless, with a look that seems to say "Poor thing!"

A step into the real world

Jordan contemplates how to orchestrate his first face-to-face meeting with Avery. He wants it to be an unforgettable moment, an occasion that transcends the simplicity of a common date. He envisions a place that can capture the essence of their virtual connection, transforming it into a tangible and even deeper reality.

He reflects on the importance of choosing the right environment, a space that can speak as much as the words that have yet to be uttered. The planning is meticulous, with the intention of creating an experience that can mark the beginning of a new phase in their story, a step from the virtual to the real, full of meaning and promises.

Avery, on the other hand, would like to meet Jordan in a public but at the same time quaint and intimate place, like a cozy cafe or one of those delightful bistros along the bay, where the atmosphere can be relaxed but meaningful.

Avery: "So it's decided. Let's choose a place halfway between us, something public yet intimate. A cafe, maybe, where we can sit, talk, and... well, just be us, without screens between us." "I like the idea. A cafe sounds perfect. It will be strange, at first, to see each other without these avatars, but I'm looking forward to it. Avery, this is our time. Let's make it happen." "I can't wait, Jordan. It will be the start of something beautiful, I'm sure. See you soon, in the real world."
Meanwhile, Jordan faces the need to invent a believable excuse for his "trip" to New York, aiming to make his arrival in the city appear as the burning desire to meet Avery in person.

With careful and discreet planning, he proposes a meeting to Avery for the following week, calculating the timing precisely so as not to arouse suspicion about the fact that he is already there. Avery, unaware and trusting in Jordan's spontaneity, accepts with enthusiasm, unable to refuse any proposal coming from him.

Meantime, Jordan, already in the city, has begun to weave the web of a silent but constant presence around Avery, without her knowledge. He has found himself in the same place where Avery stops every morning for her coffee and maple syrup waffle, walked a few meters from her as she leaves work waiting for a taxi, and on one occasion, even took a taxi to follow Avery at a distance to find out where she lived. For over two weeks, Jordan has been a shadow presence in Avery's life, always close to her without her having the slightest idea of his proximity.

During one of their usual phone calls, sharing their ideas and expectations, Jordan understands the importance for her of creating a comfortable yet safe and welcoming environment. Ultimately, he decides to embrace Avery's idea, choosing to prioritize her comfort and preferences.

Avery selects the perfect place for their meeting: a charming café not far from her home, with a familiar atmosphere. Despite its limited number of tables, the menu offers a wide variety of coffee blends from around the world, paired with a selection of artisanal pastries.

"Hi Jordan, you'll probably read this message after you arrive, but in the meantime, I'm sending you the location of the café I've chosen for our date," writes Avery. "Welcome to New York, love. Call me as soon as you can use your phone. A kiss, Avy."

In reality, Jordan is not on any flight; to keep his cover as credible as possible, he has kept his smartphone turned off for most of the day. He was returning to his studio apartment, located in the same neighborhood as Avery's office and just a 15-minute walk away.

As Avery sent the message, he passed by her unnoticed.

"I've landed, love. All is well, I'll let you know as soon as I arrive at the hotel," replies Jordan, concealing the truth with disarming ease. He likes to think of this as an act of discretion, hiding even from himself that it is pure manipulation. Avery is completely unaware that, for nearly two weeks, Jordan has been so close to her every day without ever being noticed. Perhaps, for him, it's better that way.

Avery doesn't feel the need to discuss how they might recognize each other at their first meeting. She is confident she can identify Jordan: she imagines meeting a young man with dark hair and a beard and fully trusts her ability to recognize him. Jordan, naturally, wouldn't need to ask for further details either, but his game of pretense leads him to raise the question.

"By the way, Avery, how will I recognize you? You told me that Avy doesn't look like you... so I guess I shouldn't look for a woman with red hair!" Avery plays along, replying,
"Of course not, Jordan. To keep the meeting a surprise, I'll tell you that I'll enter the café wearing a honey-colored overcoat and a blue scarf..." Jordan decides to describe his own outfit in turn:
"Well, I'll be wearing a brown leather jacket... you'll see, we'll recognize each other immediately."

Disappointments

Compared to the beginning of their virtual acquaintance, when Jordan felt apprehension about the lies regarding his appearance, he now feels completely secure in the bond they have built. He is not plagued by doubts, convinced that Avery has fallen in love with him for his voice and what it conveys, well beyond physical appearance.

In the café carefully selected for their first meeting, Avery and Jordan move in a state of excitement mixed with nervousness. He arrives at the location a full thirty minutes before the agreed time, positioning himself to wait while Avery is on her way to the place.

Upon entering, Avery scans the environment, which turns out to be unusually crowded for a Thursday evening, unable to spot any man matching the description of Jordan with a beard. Jordan, on his part, notices her as soon as she crosses the threshold but decides to observe her from afar, without intervening. After a short while, Avery leaves, believing she has not found him, and at that moment sends a message:
"Hi, I'm at the café." Jordan promptly replies:
"Me too, Avery, I'm already at the table!" With her heart in turmoil and hands damp with sweat, Avery re-enters, this time with a quickened heartbeat. She scans the room again and, in the distance, a significantly overweight man in a leather jacket gestures for her to come closer.

"Jordan?" she asks uncertainly.

"Yes, Avery, it's me!" His response leaves Avery speechless for a moment: before her is the man with whom she has shared so much, recognizable only by the voice confirming his identity.

Jordan appears without a single hair on his body, lacking hair, beard, eyelashes, and eyebrows, due to a congenital form of alopecia that leaves him completely hairless. His build is far from average weight: Avery is confronted with a young man, yes, but one with a considerably bulky body, possibly weighing between 120 and 130 kilograms. Avery's surprise is evident, clearly reflected on her face.

"Sorry, Jordan, I honestly expected someone different..." says Avery timidly, searching for the right words to express her disturbance. "Maybe you thought I would be different too," she adds, trying to lighten the mood.
"You are exactly as I had imagined," replies Jordan, despite knowing he is not being truthful.

Avery, at 48 years old, sports a look that defies the passage of time: slender and of thin build, her features are delicate and almost androgynous. Her light hair is cut short, except for a long, rebellious tuft that falls across her face, a detail she habitually tucks behind her left ear.
Her eyes, a warm amber color and surprisingly large for her age, convey a lively curiosity and a child-like innocence. Her nose is slender and well-defined, her lips slightly full but small. This feature, the small mouth, is sometimes interpreted as a symbol of vulnerability, especially in the context of relationships and social dynamics, where it might suggest less expressive or assertive communication, both verbal and nonverbal.

Interestingly, this trait is also associated with a form of egocentrism, not in a derogatory sense but as a tendency to prioritize one's own perspective and needs, sometimes highlighting a lack of emotional maturity that can resemble behaviors more typical of childhood.

Overcoming the initial embarrassment, Avery decides to break the ice. "Finally seeing you... it's incredible. You are... you're different from what I imagined," she finds herself unable to say anything more, scolding herself internally.

"Not for me... but do you know what I hadn't considered? Your scent, Avery... it's something I could never have known from afar."

Avery, with a smile on her lips, gently moves to create more distance, using the small table between them, but Jordan doesn't pick up on the nonverbal cue and continues speaking.

"... your scent is so distinctive... it seems to have been made just for you," he exclaims. Avery, visibly embarrassed by the situation, still compliments Jordan on his scent.

"*What am I saying*?" she reproaches herself mentally.

"*What situation are you getting into? Can't you see he's been mocking you all along? Why do you continue to pretend everything is okay?*" an inner voice presses her.

Jordan laughs, a clear and melodious sound that fills the air. "It's funny, isn't it? We've shared so much, and yet this closeness offers us a completely new world to explore." "*...completely new, indeed...,*" Avery reflects, still bewildered by how events have unfolded.

All her hopes crumbled in an instant.

The harsh reality was that Jordan had lied about his appearance, and who knows what else. As Jordan continued to extol the importance of their meeting, Avery felt overwhelmed with shame for having been deceived so easily, imagining the disapproving looks of Lorraine and the compassionate concern of Axel.

Avery, torn between the desire to stay or flee, had let Jordan take the initiative again, opting to order from the menu. The waiter had been waiting in front of her for a while, but Avery found it difficult to express a preference. So, Jordan makes the decision for both of them, ordering two Italian espressos and a slice of chocolate cake, Avery's favorite dessert, to share.

Avery's interest had completely vanished; she no longer had topics for conversation or questions to ask, remaining almost dazed: while Jordan continued his speech, she looked at him without really listening to what he was saying. Jordan's face was broad with a defined jawline, but there was something unusual in those features.
The eyes, nose, and mouth were small and seemed clustered in the center of the face, as if everything was compressed into a single area. The eyes appeared slightly sunken, and the mouth, lacking prominent lips, seemed closed in a rigid line when silent.

Avery remembered that, during a trip to Europe, she had ended up, she can't even recall how, at a conference on morphopsychology, the study of how a person's personality can be reflected in the traits of their face, and suddenly some concepts that might apply to Jordan's face came to mind.

Avery revisits the few concepts she learned and associates Jordan with the "dilated tonic" and "concentrated" types. In her inner examination, she recalls that, in their less favorable interpretation, individuals with these traits tend to be egocentric, show a poor ability to adapt to various circumstances, tend to overlook obstacles, not adequately consider the needs of others, and operate with an emotionally detached approach.

"And who knows what else..." Avery muses, delving into her memory for further details that could provide a deeper understanding of Jordan's character.

As he cuts a piece of cake, Jordan lifts it to Avery's lips. "Try this. It's exactly how I imagined sharing something tangible with you would be."

Avery, returning to reality, tastes the dessert, allowing the rich and intense flavors to spread.

"It's delicious…" but she finds herself unable to say more.

Jordan takes Avery's hand, exploring her skin with a light touch.

"And the touch. Remember when we talked about how much we wanted to be able to truly touch each other? Here, now we can. And it's not just the skin; it's the warmth, the real presence of you."

At that moment, everything that existed in Avery's imagination seemed to dissolve. Avery would have ardently wished that she and Jordan could fully immerse themselves in this new phase of their relationship.

The sensory exploration of touch and smell would surely have enriched their connection with unexpected depth and complexity, unveiling levels of intimacy they never thought possible. However, as deep as their bond had been until that moment, Avery felt that these experiences were beginning to lose their meaning, at least for her.

"Avery, this... all of this... is more than I ever hoped for. It's like I've known you forever, yet we're starting anew, discovering each other in ways we hadn't anticipated."

Avery remained silent, offering only a polite smile. She had never been the type of person who reacted quickly or acted decisively, even when it came to protecting herself. Jordan had understood the situation, had realized, but seemed not to care…he would convince her to stay in their relationship.

Avery's disappointment makes its way as she silently dialogues with herself, and the desire to escape from that situation grows.

Jordan is an unstoppable torrent of words; if Avery closes her eyes and focuses solely on his voice, she can almost evoke the emotions she felt interacting with him through the computer screen. However, looking into his eyes, she can no longer find her Jordan.

Finding nothing else to say or do, she decides to take a break, concocting the excuse of needing to go to the bathroom.

She walks away with determined steps and quickly closes the bathroom door behind her. There, alone, she feels the urgent need to devise a pretext to leave the place and return home, where she can calmly reflect on how to extricate herself from the situation she has created with her own hands.

"I'm sorry, Jordan, but I think it should end here. I'm disappointed. You lied to me about your appearance, and who knows what else. I now realize that in front of me is a perfect stranger. Please, don't look for me anymore, don't call me, don't write, forget about me and this absurd situation," Avery would have liked to say, once back at their table.

But the words she actually utters are quite different:

"I'm sorry, Jordan, I'm not feeling well, I need to go home. Don't worry about accompanying me, I've already called a taxi while I was in the bathroom. I'll contact you tomorrow. I have to go..."

Jordan, taken aback, can barely get up, and while he is about to put on his jacket, Avery is already outside, headed toward the taxi. Back home, her heart finally slows down, after an adrenaline rush comparable to a chase.

In front of the mirror, the two faces of Avery emerge in contrast: on one side, the compassionate part, already oppressed by guilt, scolds herself for being superficial, for judging a man solely by his appearance.

On the other, her inner voice criticizes her, calling her foolish and naive, and commands her to distance herself from the situation in the least painful way possible, leaving Jordan and the evening behind.

Feeling a desperate need to confide in someone, Avery realizes how isolated she has become over the past months, pushing away friends and family to dedicate herself exclusively to virtual relationships. Now, the feeling of loneliness overwhelming her seems almost like a just punishment for her choices, leaving her to face the consequences of her actions in deafening silence.

Jordan, still disturbed by how the events unfolded, decides to write a message to Avery.

"Hi Avy, I'm really sorry that the evening didn't go as we expected... or perhaps as you expected. I am the same man with whom you've shared thoughts and dreams in recent months, the one who knows you deeply. My feelings for you are sincere; I truly believe I love you and am ready to do anything for you. After all this time and everything we've shared, I wish to at least have the chance to prove to you that what I feel is real. Please, give me the chance to be part of your life in a concrete and tangible way."

The sound of the notification on Avery's phone, once awaited and desired, now seems unbearable to her. In a gesture of frustration, she throws her smartphone against the wall.

The night proves to be endless; Avery, staring at the ceiling, feels empty and exhausted from lack of sleep. Jordan, who initially thought of going to her house, realizes that perhaps this is not the time to push further. He had underestimated the extent of Avery's reaction.

It's true, their relationship had always developed away from reality, a face-to-face meeting had never been considered, and this seemed to pose no problem in their virtual world. However, real life has turned out to be a very different context.

Avery gets out of bed and rushes to check her phone, fearing that her previous night's fury might have damaged it. Fortunately, she finds only a few scratches on the screen, but the battery is almost completely dead. Before venturing into any applications, she decides to put it on the wireless charger.

She gets ready slowly, with no urgency, skipping breakfast because she feels no need for it. She knows Jordan has sent her some messages and almost fears the idea of having to read them.

She can't fathom how quickly one's feelings towards someone can change.

She then has to admit to herself an uncomfortable truth: if Jordan had presented his true appearance from the beginning, she probably would never have been interested in him.

For Avery, the image is as important as the essence; both form and content matter. The idea of judging someone solely by their "inner beauty" has always seemed to her not only naive but decidedly absurd.

Avery finally decides to make that phone call.

"Axel?"

"Avery? Is everything okay?" Axel's voice is laced with concern and surprise. Avery hesitates, feeling almost guilty for turning to him for advice, but sees no other options.

"I'm fine, Axel, I just needed to talk to someone..."

"Avery, did something happen with Eric? I didn't act my best last time, I'm sorry!"
"No, it's not about Eric, it's about... Jordan," she responds.
"Tell me," presses Axel, his curiosity mixed with a hint of jealousy.

"Last night we met for the first time, and I couldn't express to him what I really thought..."
"Meaning?" asks Axel, increasingly intrigued.

"It might sound ridiculous to you, but I got completely carried away with this story, living it as if it were real. Only now do I understand how easy it is to fall into these illusions... I don't know what got into me, the idea that I could fall in love with someone just for their well-phrased words. Meeting with an avatar, no less! Can you be more foolish than that?!" Avery vents her frustration and disappointment, only now realizing the naivety of her behavior.

"I don't exactly know what you want me to say, Avery. You got yourself into this situation, and now you have to find a way out. Don't get me wrong, I wish I could help, but for your own sake, you need to solve this problem!" Axel responds in a neutral tone, trying to keep his emotions in check.

"You're an adult woman, not a little girl. I'm sure you'll find a way to free yourself from this guy who thinks he's in love with you..." and he adds, "When you decide to cut ties with someone, you're more than capable of doing it!" Avery reflects on Axel's words and can't help but think she deserved that response.

A new appointment

Avery is immersed in her thoughts, wrapped in her sweater, sitting in front of the large window of her apartment. She appears thinner than usual, her gaze fixed on the phone screen open to her chat with Jordan, where his last message still awaits a response. She is so absorbed that the sound of the intercom catches her by surprise, ringing a second time before she reacts.

"Axel?" she exclaims, incredulous, looking at the video intercom.
"Can I come up?" he asks, with his usual politeness.
"Yes, of course," responds Avery, quickly fixing her hair in the entrance mirror. The sleepless night has left its mark on her face, where some new tension wrinkles are noticeable.

"Hi Avery," Axel greets her with a hug,
"I'm really sorry for how I was last night: I didn't act as you had hoped, I wasn't the friend I should have been... And now I'm here because, thinking back on what you told me, I've started to have doubts." Without giving Avery time to interject, he continues as if afraid of forgetting what he had to say.
"You told me that throughout your online relationship you never met in person, right?" Avery nods.
"He's practically a stranger to you, but you, Avery, are a known art critic; are you sure he hasn't researched you? That he doesn't know how you look or where you live and work?" Axel poses these questions with an urgent tone, almost to emphasize the seriousness of his concerns.

"I don't know," replies Avery with a tone laden with uncertainty.

"I never thought about it, actually... How foolish of me! Yes, it would have been really easy for Jordan to find out who I am. He deceived me all along." She berates herself, repeating: "How foolish, how foolish!"

"Don't talk like that," Axel interjects gently.
"You were simply excited about this new acquaintance and felt so protected behind your computer that you let your guard down," he continues.
"I'm sure that in different circumstances, your intuition would have kicked in much earlier."

"Still, Axel, these remain just assumptions. We can't be sure that things are really like this," Avery replies.

"Well, Avery, there's only one way to find out... You need to see him again and force him to tell you the truth, about himself, about your relationship..." suggests Axel, proposing a direct confrontation with Jordan to clear up any doubts.

"I can't even imagine seeing him now, Axel," replies Avery, her voice full of reluctance.

"I understand," continues Axel, undeterred,
"but you can't leave things hanging without having all the answers. Try to arrange another meeting with him. I'll be there with you; you won't be alone. It's crucial that you find out the truth, so you won't have these doubts in the future and can live peacefully!"

"As always, Axel, you manage to make me see things from another perspective, and I can only agree with you... but I accept on the condition that you'll be there with me. Your presence makes me feel protected." Avery grabs her phone and composes a message to Jordan:

"Hi, I feel the need to see you again to clarify some things. Last night I was overwhelmed by emotions and wasn't ready. Let's meet tonight at the usual café at 6 pm. Avery"

Jordan was trying to devise a plan to regain Avery's trust when his phone vibrates with a new message.

"Thank you, Avery. I too feel the need to see you again. I hope I can dispel your doubts. Hugs, see you tonight," he responds quickly, a whirlwind of agitated emotions assailing him. The feeling of losing her is tangible, but he still sees a chance for redemption.

"I must act smartly," he thinks, "after all, she's a woman who is alone, in love with the idea of love more than with herself. It shouldn't be hard to win her back."

Meanwhile, Axel organizes with Avery: he will already be seated inside the café before her arrival, ready to discreetly monitor the meeting. Determined to protect her, he won't allow Jordan to make any move that could hurt her.

As the time of the appointment approaches, Jordan prepares and decides to bring tulips, Avery's favorite flowers, and tries to muster all his best phrases of apology: "Forgive me," "You're the only one I've truly loved," "There will be no more lies between us," hoping they might soften Avery's heart. She, for her part, mentally reviews all the questions she intends to ask, determined to obtain sincere and complete answers, without interruptions.

Upon entering the café, Jordan immediately notices Axel. His research on Avery had revealed a photo of the two together at an award ceremony, and he had figured that their paths would eventually cross.

The apparent indifference with which Axel sips his coffee, pretending to be engrossed in his smartphone, does not fool Jordan; he knows he is there for Avery.

When Avery and Jordan finally face each other, the impact with reality is harsh. Avery's forced smile and her effort to maintain a conversation clash with the harsh truth: the person before her is not the one she had idealized. Their once fluid and engaging chats have given way to prolonged and awkward silences.

"Avery, you're beautiful," Jordan starts, but she, with a demeanor of firm determination, interrupts to deliver the speech she has carefully prepared.

"Jordan, listen carefully and do not interrupt me. You will only have the opportunity to speak when I ask you direct questions, and please answer truthfully. If I sense even a hint of a lie, I will get up and leave," Avery declares with a firmness surprising even to herself.

"I am deeply disappointed. I believed in us, in our story. The fact that our relationship was only online never made me doubt its authenticity. I never thought it was acceptable to lie. It's clear you deceived me about your appearance, but what's more disconcerting is that I never saw a look of surprise in your eyes... Because, in fact, you had nothing to be surprised about since you already knew everything about me. You knew what I looked like, right? Your questions about my physical appearance were just a way to avoid raising my suspicions, weren't they? I don't understand... in the end, you were the one pushing for this in-person meeting. Did you really think you had nothing to fear? That I wouldn't react? That I would pretend nothing happened?"

Jordan realizes that Avery has sensed the truth, he finds himself cornered, aware that he cannot retreat into his usual arsenal of rhetoric and platitudes. With a thin voice, he knows he must face the situation honestly.

"Yes, Avery, I knew a lot about you. I looked up photos and information online to understand your tastes and get a better sense of who you are, all in the hope of gaining your trust. But I assure you, everything we shared was authentic to me!" The tension that had oppressed Avery dissolves into a bitter laugh.

"Authentic? Do you really understand the weight of that word? Nothing was authentic, maybe not even us, at this precise moment..."

A dull noise abruptly interrupts her sleep. The water bottle she had left on the nightstand has fallen, accidentally pushed over as she moved the pillow away with a sweep.

Reality

Avery wakes up from a restless sleep, emerged from a dream so bitter that she struggles to distinguish reality from fiction. Confused, she sits up and grabs her phone: the last message sent to Jordan talks about a strange dream, increasing her perplexity.

She heads to the kitchen for a glass of water and notices, through the slightly ajar door of the study, a pile of boxes. They contain Eric's things... With her mind still foggy, she frantically searches for her PC, the DreamLens viewer, the webcam, the haptic suit, and the glove, but finds nothing. *"Impossible,"* she thinks, as a growing sense of altered reality overwhelms her.

She checks her phone again and finds a message from Tessa asking to meet in the office to sign some documents. *"No, it can't be, I had already signed them..."* she murmurs. She logs onto the computer and checks: there is no trace of any software for accessing virtual worlds, in the messages from Jordan the Simply Red song is missing, which was also the soundtrack of her relationship with Eric. There is nothing, absolutely nothing that confirms her experiences. Everything that seemed so tangible, so real, turns out to be an illusion.

Yet, amidst this turmoil, she finds a small comfort in realizing that even the night of love with Axel, the clash between him and Eric, and the disappointing encounter with Jordan were not real.

They were just the fruit of her imagination, a journey through her dream world or perhaps some unexplored parallel universe. Reality, as confusing and elusive as it may be, offers her an anchor of salvation: the chance to start over, free from the chains of an experience that, although intensely lived, never actually took place.

As Avery tries to untangle the threads of her memory, attempting to discern what actually happened and rejecting the notion that it could have all been just a dream, her cell phone vibrates with a new notification: a message from Jordan.

"Hi Avery,

I hope this day is bringing you smiles. As I reflected on new ways to explore and deepen our connection, an idea occurred to me that I hope you'll find intriguing.

Have you ever heard of virtual environments like NeoHorizon? These are virtual worlds where people can create avatars to explore identities, relationships, and experiences in creative and new ways. I was wondering... what would you say to venturing together into this virtual space? It could be a fun and safe way to experiment with different aspects of our personality and our relationships, all within a controlled and liberating environment.

Through avatars, we could experience romantic moments together, or even just exploratory ones, in scenarios that would be impossible or impractical in real life. I think it could be a unique opportunity to get to know each other better, in a context different from the usual, and perhaps discover new sides of each other.

Sure, the proposal might seem a bit unusual, but I believe it could be an exciting experience for both of us. And who knows, maybe we'll find surprising ways to interact and express our feelings in this parallel world.

Let me know what you think. If the idea intrigues you, I'm here to explore this new universe together with you. And, of course, if you prefer to keep our interactions as they are now, that's perfectly fine with me too. The most important thing for me is that we feel comfortable and happy in our relationship, whatever form it may take.

I eagerly await your response.

Warm regards,
Jordan"

With growing wonder, Avery realizes she has encountered messages of this nature before, recalling with precision the circumstances that had led her to embrace that proposal in the past.

She finds herself in a situation that gives her the impression of reliving events she has already experienced, as if she had jumped into the future and now had the key to understand every impending development. Before her is the unusual opportunity to alter the course of events.

"If the universe has decided to play this joke on me, there must be a reason," reflects Avery, seeing the hidden potential behind this unexpected repetition.
Illuminated by the awareness of events that have already unfolded once, Avery opts for a different response to Jordan's message, declining his offer to dive into the virtual world and instead proposing to reconsider the option of a video call. She is determined to meet him again, this time to peer beyond the surface of things, to see if this change in mode can somehow alter the dynamic between them.
But above all, Avery wants to look him in the eyes, to confront the reality of Jordan, questioning whether the man she will meet will be the same one who populated her dream.

This need to clarify her doubts, to verify the truthfulness of their connection beyond the digital illusion, becomes an urgency she can no longer ignore.

"Hi Jordan,

I received your message and, I must admit, your proposal to explore virtual environments like NeoHorizon has sparked some reflection in me. The idea of immersing ourselves in such an innovative world and discovering new dimensions of our personalities through avatars and digital scenarios is undoubtedly intriguing.

After much thought, however, I have realized that this experience might not be what I am looking for at this point in my life. The prospect of navigating these virtual spaces, while a fascinating frontier, has led me to reflect on what I truly desire from our interaction and our relationship.

I believe my quest for connection with you, and with people in general, is more rooted in tangible reality, in face-to-face exchanges that allow us to immediately perceive each other's emotions and reactions. It is in these moments of shared presence that I truly feel connected, where the unspoken words are as eloquent as those uttered.

Therefore, with all due respect for your proposal and recognizing the value it might hold for others, I must decline the invitation to join in this virtual adventure.

I hope you do not take this decision as a rejection of the possibility of exploring and growing together, but rather as a personal choice towards the type of experiences that I feel would enrich me more at this moment.

I sincerely thank you for considering me for this digital journey and for your understanding. I hope we can find other ways to continue getting to know each other and develop our bond in ways that authentically resonate with both of us.

With affection,
Avery"

Avery feels a sense of relief mixed with a sense of power she never thought possible. She has the opportunity to shape her present and forge a different future. With a flicker of hope, she ardently wishes that this time it's not all just a dream. After sending the message, she calls Tessa:

"Good morning, Tessa. I will come to the office to sort out the paperwork in the afternoon. I'll be there after lunch."

Next, Avery picks up her phone again and sends a message to Eric:
"Hi, please arrange to pick up your things this afternoon. I'll leave the keys with the doorman, and you can return them once you're done." Avery feels satisfied; this way, she avoids having to meet him and can finally clear her home of the negative energy accumulated. She truly feels as if she has been reborn, activating a series of strategic actions to free herself from her anxieties and the silences that have long oppressed her. A new Avery is taking shape, ready to face life with renewed determination and clarity.

"I need to meet Axel," Avery reflects, determined. "It's essential to find out if his feelings for me stem from an illusion or if there is a basis in reality." With this determination, she sends a message:

"Hi Axel, how are you?"

"Hi Avery, yes, all good. And you, how are you doing?"
"Never been better," Avery replies, with a smile Axel can almost sense through the words.

"I'd like to talk to you, do you have time for lunch today?"
"Absolutely, Avery. Would you like to go back to the bistro on the beach? I remember you enjoyed it."

"Yes, that would be ideal. This time though, let's go for beach attire, so we can take a walk along the shore."

"Alright, see you there. But... are you sure everything's okay? You seem unusually enthusiastic."

With these words, Avery confirms the meeting, feeling charged with new energy and ready to clarify Axel's feelings towards her, hoping to find the answers she seeks.

Meanwhile, Jordan reads Avery's message and finds himself engulfed in a sea of doubts. He ponders what she really wants: does she want to keep her distance, or is she interested in continuing their relationship?
He realizes that to make things work between them, it's necessary to find an effective way to communicate and interact. At the same time, he can't help but fear that he asked too much, too soon, risking scaring her with his proposal to explore the metaverse together.
He reflects on how venturing into such a new and unknown world can be intimidating at first for those without direct experience.

Meanwhile, under the warm sun illuminating the beach, Avery and Axel find a spot in the cozy bistro, with the sea breeze slightly tousling their hair. Avery, with a mix of excitement and nervousness, prepares to share with Axel the content of her strange dream and the reflections that followed.

"Axel, I need to talk to you about a dream I had," begins Avery, trying to find the right words. "It was so intense and realistic that it left me confused when I woke up."

Axel listens attentively, encouraging her to continue with a nod.

"In this dream, maybe a parallel world, I had experiences that made me reflect on us... on you," Avery continues, searching his eyes for a sign.
"And it made me realize how much I value our friendship, Axel. But it also made me question the nature of your feelings."

Axel remains silent for a moment, then speaks calmly. "Avery, dreams can be powerful. I'm glad to hear they've led you to think about us. And I want you to know that whatever you feel or decide, I'll be here for you." Gently, she decides to invite Axel to share his deepest feelings, hoping to create a space where he can feel free to open up.

"Axel," Avery starts, her voice imbued with intentional sweetness, "this dream I had... it's made me think a lot about us. About how we relate and what we feel for each other." Her expression is inviting, encouraging, as she locks eyes with him, seeking a deeper connection.

Axel seems hesitant, but the atmosphere of sincerity Avery has created invites him to let go.

"Avery, I must admit that I've thought about it too," he responds softly, almost surprised by his own candor.

Avery gently takes his hand, a gesture of support and encouragement.

"Axel, whatever you feel, it's important to me. Our friendship is precious, but I also want you to know that you're free to express anything that's on your mind, without fear."

Axel's face lights up with a shy but sincere smile.

"Avery, you are an incredible person, and the time we've spent together has made me realize how much I appreciate you... not just as a friend. It's true, I have feelings for you that go beyond friendship. But the most important thing for me is to maintain our bond, whatever form it may take."

Avery listens intently, moved by his sincerity.
"Thank you, Axel, for sharing this with me. Your honesty means a lot. And I want you to know that, regardless of how things evolve between us, your friendship will always be a treasure to me."

Avery exhales, relieved, and continues,
"Axel, what I've realized is that I care a lot about you and our friendship. And, although the dream mixed up my feelings, I want our relationship to remain on this level."

Axel smiles reassuringly.
"Avery, your friendship is also precious to me. And if this is what you wish, then I am happy to continue walking by your side as a friend."

They allow themselves a moment of silence, contemplating the sea in front of them. Then Avery, with a light smile, suggests:
"How about a walk on the beach? I think it would do us good."

"Agreed, Avery. Let's walk," responds Axel, accepting the invitation.

As they walk along the shore, the words shared between them strengthen the bond of friendship that unites them, a bond that both appreciate and wish to preserve. The conversation flows freely, and Avery feels grateful for Axel's presence in her life, aware that, despite the dream leading her to question things, the reality of their friendship is something tangible and precious.

A new beginning

The lunch with Axel left Avery with a lightness in her heart. *"Clarifying things with Axel was liberating,"* she reflects as she heads to the office, feeling as if a weight has been lifted from her shoulders.

"Every piece of the puzzle is finding its place..." This realization allows her to dedicate herself to the afternoon's work with a clear mind, focusing fully on organizing the exhibition.

"Jordan is undeniably a talented artist, deserving of recognition, regardless of what happens between us," Avery thinks.

"If I could change the course of events, if I could alter what happened, perhaps both of us could aspire to a better future."

Jordan's phone rings, signaling a call from Avery.

"Hello Jordan," Avery begins, "I assume you've read my message."

"Hello Avery, yes, I read it and I must admit, it left me a bit perplexed," he replies, confusion evident in his voice.

"I understand... Lately, my behavior may seem a bit erratic, but I intend to clarify things," Avery states, determined to resolve the situation. However, she is aware that she cannot reveal to Jordan the true nature of her dream or her dreamlike experience, to not appear insane to him.

Suddenly, Avery suggests,

"How about we switch this call to a video call?" Jordan immediately agrees, though he remains filled with questions and a palpable sense of confusion. Avery hopes that, seeing each other face-to-face, even through a screen, can dispel all her doubts and perhaps find a way to move forward, breaking the strange spell of the dream.

"Finally, we can see each other," Jordan begins, trying to mask some embarrassment. Avery, with a mix of surprise and recognition, stares at the screen where Jordan appears. He is in his unique state, hairless due to congenital alopecia, lacking hair, beard, eyelashes, and eyebrows.

"I can't believe it," Avery thinks, offering him a forced smile. "It's really him, the Jordan of my dream... I knew it." With some effort, she manages to say, "Well..here I am."

Jordan, in turn, observes Avery, a woman in her fifties with short, light hair, except for a long, unruly tuft that slips over her face. Her eyes, a deep amber color, are surprisingly expressive and large, her nose delicate, and her lips, though small, are rather full.

"It's nice to see you, Avery," says Jordan, trying to disguise a slight discomfort.
"I must admit, I had a different image of you in mind... I don't know why, but I imagined you with dark hair. However, your eyes... they are exactly as I had dreamed."

Avery, surprised yet composed, responds:
"And I, honestly, never imagined you like this. But it's good, you know? We can finally put a face to our voices." Her voice conveys a mix of surprise and acceptance as she observes Jordan, noting how reality differs from her expectations and how, despite this, there is something positively surprising about finally seeing the person behind their exchanged words.

During the video call, Avery and Jordan find a pleasant rhythm in their conversation, touching on various topics, and despite the initial awkwardness, both relax, recognizing the value of their connection, albeit in a context different from what they had imagined.

"Jordan, you have a unique talent, and I think the contemporary art world absolutely needs to discover it."

"Thank you, Avery. That means a lot to me, especially coming from you. I've always feared not measuring up or not finding my place in this competitive field."

"I understand your concerns, but believe me, you have something special. That's why I'd like to help you organize your first exhibition. I think we have the opportunity to create something truly unique."

"I really don't know how to thank you. It would be a dream come true. But... what about us? What will happen between us?"

"Jordan, I think it's important to be honest with each other. What we've shared so far has been important and taught me a lot. However, I feel that for now, our relationship should stay exactly where it is. We can be great friends and collaborators. I believe working together on your artistic projects could be incredibly rewarding for both of us, without having to complicate things on other fronts."

"It will take me some time to get used to the idea, but I respect your decision. And I am sincerely grateful for your support and the opportunity to work together. Who knows? Perhaps this collaboration will open new doors for both of us."

"Exactly, Jordan. And who can say where these projects will lead us? The important thing is that we remain open to possibilities and support each other, as friends and as colleagues."

"Avery, thank you. I'm ready to see where this new adventure will take us. And who knows... maybe the best is yet to come!"

The call ends with a sense of mutual understanding and respect.

Avery has found the strength within herself not to be overwhelmed by loneliness, a personal victory that gives her new vigor.

She has shaped not only her future but also those of Axel and Jordan, altering the course of events. This unusual miracle has offered her the chance to look with new eyes at the potential directions of her life, filling her with a deep sense of gratitude.

Meanwhile, Eric, leaving Avery's apartment with a load of boxes and documents, experiences a minor mishap: one of the boxes overturns, scattering its contents on the sidewalk. Initially convinced that everything he was carrying was his, he realizes the mistake as soon as he bends down to pick up the fallen items.

"This must belong to Avery," he reasons, noticing a VR headset, a webcam, and a haptic suit among the scattered objects.